ON ROUTE 66

Also by Daniel Wyatt

Two Wings and a Prayer
Maximum Effort
The Last Flight of the Arrow
The Mary Jane Mission
The Cotton Run
Pennant Man
Route 66

"The Falcon File" series:
The Fuehrermaster
The Filberg Consortium
Foo Fighters

ON ROUTE 66

Twelve Stories on Route 66

Daniel Wyatt

Published by
Bladud Books

First published in Great Britain in 2015 by Mushroom eBooks

This Paperback edition published in 2018 by
Bladud Books, an imprint of Mushroom Publishing,
Bath, BA1 4EB, United Kingdom

www.bladudbooks.com

ISBN 978-1-84319-493-4

Contents

Prologue

It was only a road. But. . . *what a road*. Route 66 was the first of its kind. A kind of continental avenue, a two-lane stretch of highway birthed on the south shore of Lake Michigan, concluding at the Pacific. As the railroad had linked the United States in the late 1800s and opened up the west to settlers, Route 66 too opened the west—mainly California—to the automobile traffic of the new century. Completed in 1926, Route 66 ran from Chicago to Los Angeles, over 2400 miles of sightseeing adventure through the Ozarks, the bald prairie, farmers' fields, rock, and desert. It covered eight states and three time zones. The Land of Lincoln. The Show Me State. Bloody Kansas. The Lone Star State. The High Country. The Mojave Desert. People packed up and left the east. Next stop, the Sunshine State. Paved completely by 1938, U.S. Route 66 had reached a new plateau and became a fully-modern federal highway.

The entrepreneurs came in droves and built their businesses along the highway. Diners, motels, reptile ranches, fireworks shops and maple syrup stands. The gas companies put up their filling stations. All to service the traveling public. The 1950s saw the heyday of U.S. Route 66. The era spawned faster cars and more time on peoples' hands. Meanwhile. . . in Washington, President Dwight D. Eisenhower—elected in 1953—brought to mind the four-lane German autobahn he had seen while stationed in Europe as Supreme Commander of the Allied Forces during World War II. In his first White House term, he introduced legislation that would set the gears in motion for contractors to construct a series of four-lane superhighways linking the west to the east, as well as the north to the south. It was the beginning of the end of Route 66. The interstates came, and by 1984 the last stretch of the ol' 66 was decertified.

Over the years Route 66 has been immortalized three specific times. First, the 1940s *Grapes of Wrath* movie referred to it as the Mother Road, the roadway to the land of *milk and honey*. . . that is California. Second, in song written by Bobby Troup in 1946 and recorded numerous times since. And third, the Route 66 television series starring Martin Milner, George Maharis, and later Glenn Corbett.

To this day, Route 66 is remembered fondly by those who drove it. Greasy hamburgers in diners, the snowstorms through the mountain passes, the towns along the way and the Pacific Ocean at the west end of it all. Although most of it can still be driven, the road is not found on any road map. Locals only know it as Historic Route 66. Gone, but not forgotten. However, organizations are keeping the memory of the Mother Road alive in the eight states that had seen its traffic from the beginning.

This book is dedicated to the legendary road. It's a book about people. People on the move. *On Route 66* is a series of short stories that cover that great and wonderful era in the good ol' US of A, when the open road brought something new, exciting, and magical around every corner and bend. Everyone always wants to see what's on the other side of the hill.

1

Just a Hunch

The Roaring Twenties was one of those memorable, yet strange decades, a mixture of flappers and jazz music, mobsters and prohibition, and stocks and speculators. Herbert Hoover was president. World War I, the war to end all wars, had come to a peace-loving end in late 1918. The boys were back home, whooping it up. People were carefree and wild. The daring engaged in flagpole sitting, barnstorming, and marathon dances. The even-more-daring spent money they really didn't have. Never mind tomorrow. By 1929, the last year of this mayhem, something ominous loomed on the horizon. Some—the smart ones—saw it coming. But most didn't.

CHICAGO—OCTOBER, 1929

Honeymooners Jake and Jennifer Courtney were oblivious to what they were in for as they stepped off the New York-to-Chicago train in mid-afternoon on a chilly, rainy Tuesday to flag down a cab on the street outside the station.

"Where to?"

"The Royal Palace Hotel," Jake answered the driver.

"Yes, sir."

They squeezed in the cab's back seat. The driver whipped the couple's luggage into the trunk and spun off. Along the way, Jake and Jennifer caught the sights of the busy town they had heard so much about, on this day off between train connections for the western leg of their honeymoon trip to sunny California. The streets in the Loop were packed with people and cars, despite the heavy rain. Exciting place, this Chicago, according to the talkative cab driver. People—mostly outsiders—called it the Windy City. It had over a million people. One writer called it "the pulse of America." It was an ethnic city of many nationalities. Poles, Germans, Jews, Italians, and Irish. All trying to get along, despite their differences. It was a city of factories and slaughter houses. On the dark side, it was also a city of speakeasies and the notorious Al Capone. The Courtneys nodded at the driver. Who hadn't heard of Al Capone?

An attractive couple in their early twenties, the Courtneys hailed from New York City, an even bigger jungle than Chicago. Jake was dark-haired, six-foot-two, handsome, and fashionably-dressed. Jennifer was a pretty blonde with slim legs who loved her hats and thrived on attention. Some thought of her as a classy little wench. High-class, high-esteem. Despite a stormy courtship, they were a twosome. Hopefully for life. However, few relatives wondered to themselves whether they'd be lucky to last five years. Both also had money in the family. Jake's father owned a large, popular department store in downtown Manhattan. Jennifer's father was a Wall Street stockbroker in a firm he had helped establish in a three-way partnership. Married only three days earlier in a mammoth Catholic service attended by the New York mayor, the Courtneys were out to see America coast to coast before settling down to married life in New York, where Jake would begin his new position in his father's company as head of personnel.

But for now, they had made up their minds they wanted to make the most of their honeymoon in the quickest time possible.

"There you go," Jake said, tipping the cab driver by the curb at the *Royal Palace Hotel* on State Street.

"Five bucks. Thanks, pal," the driver said, almost expecting the amount.

The couple bent down, snatched up their luggage and hurried their way into the spacious lobby, trying not to get soaked from the pelting rain.

"Do you think we'll see a real live gangster?" Jennifer asked, flicking rain off her forehead with her free hand.

He stared at her. "Quiet. Not so loud."

"Why?"

"What do you want? Another St. Valentine's Day Massacre?"

She laughed, bringing to mind the gory newspaper accounts of the much-written-about February gang killing in Chicago. "No, I don't. But I thought you said some gangsters hang out here. Isn't that what you said?"

"The clerk at the train station said they did."

"Oh, her. The brunette with the big chest and low IQ."

"I didn't really notice her."

"Oh, yes, *you did.*"

"Anyway, so what about gangsters? As long as they don't bother us." They checked in at the front desk.

Ten minutes later, at Room 313, Jake tipped the bellhop two dollars. "I'll take over. We're newlyweds."

"I understand. Thank you, sir."

"You're welcome."

Jake placed the suitcases inside the door and flipped his wife off her feet and into his arms.

"Again?" she giggled. "You did this once before."

"I know."

She caught the twinkle in his eye. "I guess it was a long trip."

"*Oh, yes.*" Two days in the coach. No sleeping quarters. Some honeymoon. Oh, yes, too long of a trip for two people just married. "Pucker up," he demanded.

She smacked him a quick hard kiss on the lips. "Take that."

Jake whisked her inside and shut the door with a kick. The beige-colored room had a separate bedroom from the other quarters. He walked with her in his arms to the bed and set her down. He whipped her shoes off. They bounced on the bed, undressed each other in record time until they were completely naked, and then ran for the shower, together.

Jennifer heard her husband talking to someone beyond the closed door. Was someone else in their room? She sat up in bed on one elbow and pulled the covers over her bare breasts. A funny feeling cut deep inside her. She tried to make out the conversation, but couldn't quite distinguish the words. It seemed one-sided. Only Jake was doing the talking.

She heard the click of the telephone receiver. Then silence.

Jake returned to the bedroom, clad in a bathrobe, a bottle of red wine and two glasses in his hand. "Oh, hi, doll."

"Hi."

"You woke up," he said. He managed a grin. "Care for some wine?"

"I thought it was illegal?"

He laughed. "Anything goes here in Chicago."

"Where'd yuh get it?"

"Don't ask." He held up the bottle, "Well?"

"Let her rip."

He poured for her, then him.

She dropped the covers to expose her bare chest. They smiled at each other.

"Nice," he said, kissing her round, ample breasts.

They clinked glasses and downed a good mouthful. Then he went to the dresser for his cigarettes and matches.

She crawled back under the covers. "What was that all about?"

"What?"

"You were talking to someone."

He shrugged, lighting his cigarette. "Oh. . . ah. . . that. Yeah, my dad in New York."

"How is he? Anything wrong?"

He approached the bed again. "Fine."

"So, why did you call him?"

"To let him know we made it safe and sound." He stood and blew out a perfect smoke ring. "Why the questions, anyway?"

"Just curious."

"Don't be, OK?"

"OK."

"Yuh hungry?"

"Yeah, I'm starved."

"Get dressed. Let's go down to the restaurant."

"I'm with you."

She reached for her black panties and bra on the floor, while he left for the restroom. Putting on her underclothes and nylons, she decided

6

to let the telephone conversation go for now. Still, something didn't sit well with her.

The next morning turned out sunny and mild. After breakfast, another strange thing occurred. Instead of heading for the train station, Jake asked the cabby to take them to a Western Union office. Jake flew inside and out again in minutes, while his wife remained inside the cab. Next stop was a Pierce Arrow car dealer five blocks away, where the driver left them standing with their suitcases before he sped off into the steady stream of jammed traffic.

"What are we doing here?" she asked.

"You'll see." Jake took her by the hand into the showroom. There, he saw a sparkling, red convertible in the corner.

In an instant, a salesman in his forties was on them.

"May I help you?"

"Yes, you may. How much for the 4-Passenger Tourer?"

"Jake!"

"Take it easy," Jake said to his wife.

"*Ah. . .* you have good taste, sir."

"How much?"

The salesman looked towards the vehicle, than back to Jake. "The straight-eight. Water-cooled. Four forward gears. Cast iron heads and block. Three hundred and eighty-six cubic inches. One hundred and twenty-five horsepower at your pedal. Twenty-four gallon gas tank. One hundred and thirty-four inch wheelbase. She's a beaut."

"Yeah, yeah. OK, cut the shit, pal. One last time. How much?"

The salesman tugged at his tie. "The showroom price is two thousand, nine hundred dollars."

"I see. I'll give you two thousand, seven hundred in cash, providing I can drive it out of here in an hour." Jake couldn't figure whose eyes were wider, the salesman's or his wife's. "Well?"

"You mean to tell me you're carrying around that much cash in Chicago?"

"Right now I am."

"All right, I'll go see what I can do."

"We'll wait. We're not going anywhere."

Less than fifty-five minutes later, the couple were standing in the parking lot next to their spontaneous purchase.

7

"Where did you get the money?" she asked, opening the passenger side door to admire the plush, black leather interior.

"At the Western Union."

"I know that, but. . . where. . . who?"

"It doesn't matter."

"Why not?"

"Leave it be."

"Don't you think we should discuss these things?"

"OK. I had it saved."

"What?"

"I love it." He slid in behind the wheel and looked over the dash at the long, red hood. Under the shiny metal was a straight-eight motor with lots of horsepower. "I always wanted a new Pierce Arrow."

"You *saved* it?"

"Huh? Yeah, a secret account."

She frowned. "A secret account? Which one?"

"Why is everything you say turning out to be a question? Actually, my dad gave me the money. *OK?* Come on, get in. Don't be shy."

There, his father mentioned, again, she thought. She got in and slammed the door behind her. "Why a car? We're taking the train to California, aren't we?"

He shook his head. "Not no more, doll. We're driving."

She went very still as if in a trance. "Wait a minute, here!" she erupted. "Driving! Are you crazy? Do you realize how far it is to California!"

"Yeah, Chicago to Los Angeles is about twenty-four hundred miles."

She rolled her eyes. "Jake!"

"Relax, doll. Look." He reached into the breast pocket of his black, pin-striped suit and handed her a newspaper article he had torn from the *Chicago Times*.

"What's this?"

"Read it. Go on."

Jennifer unfolded the sheet. It was a full-page story with a picture of a mountain scene off in the distance. In the forefront was a paved highway. To the right a gas station. "*Route 66.*"

"That's her. The Main Street of America. I like that. The Main Street of America."

"So?"

"*So?* It's the road of the future. Starts right here in downtown Chicago—a few blocks from here on Jackson Boulevard—and goes all the way to Los Angeles. It covers eight states. Missouri, Texas, Oklahoma, Arizona. . ."

"Is it safe?"

"*Is it safe?* People travel it all the time. Been around for three years now," he explained.

"Where would we stay?"

"Major hotels in the bigger cities. They have tourist cabins in the country. Says so in the article. We'll rough it. Single room with a bed. Showers in a separate building. Outhouses."

"Outhouses! Not on your life. I might get slivers, or worse, some. . . some disease!"

"Oh, ease up, doll. Too proud, are yuh, to set your sweet little white fanny down on an outdoor toilet? Come on, it'll be an adventure. A big camp-out."

"*Oh yeah,* like. . . the Oregon Trail in a chuck wagon."

"It'll be a milk run. You'll see."

"I somehow doubt that." Looking down, she began to read portions of the article. The more she read, however, the more she liked the idea of driving all the way to the Pacific coast. She had never done or even thought of doing anything like this before.

"What do you say? Sounds like fun," he said. "We'll see places we've never been before. We can go to the Grand Canyon!"

"I've always wanted to see the Grand Canyon."

"Atta, girl."

"How long will it take?"

"A week, I suspect. Remember, that's one way."

"Do we have money?"

"I have some left over. Enough to get us there and back, with some to spare."

She glanced again at the newspaper article. "Says here that most of it isn't paved yet. Let's see. A little in Oklahoma. Not at all in Texas!"

"Big deal."

"Yeah, but. . . what if the car conks out?"

"What if we get hit by a street car in New York when we go to work? Does anybody think of those things? No. Well?"

"Well, what?"

"We going or what?"

She shook her head. *How much cash was he carrying?* "It's just that you hit me with this all of a sudden."

"We can't back out now. We got the car."

"Ah. . . why not," she said, caving in.

"That's my girl."

"I don't like that look," she said.

"You know, we could have sex in every state."

"Really." She swatted him on the shoulder.

"What? It didn't cross your mind?"

She smirked. "You know, we'll need some good road maps."

"Easy. We'll grab them along the way."

And so the adventure began.

They threw the suitcases in the trunk and off they drove through the downtown Loop and Cicero and didn't set their feet on solid ground again until they reached a country diner outside Joliet. The Weaver Inn was a tidy establishment with red gingham tablecloths, fancy laminated menus and friendly service.

In the middle of their hot, roast beef lunches, Jake suddenly came to his feet. "I have to go to the restroom," he said, and hurried down the hall.

I guess he really had to go, Jennifer mused. She didn't think anything peculiar until she finished her lunch to the last crumb and her second cup of coffee. Meanwhile, Jake still hadn't returned. Something was strange. So, she wiped her mouth and went looking for him. She made her way to the hall where the restrooms were located and then, out of the corner of her eye, she spotted Jake through the hall window. He was at a telephone booth next to the building, his back to her.

What was he doing now?

She opened the hall door slowly and heard the words. "Yes, do it. . . I said do it. . . No, I won't wait. . . do it. . . And don't tell you-know-who. Anyway, I gotta go. Jennifer will wonder where I've been."

That's an understatement, Jennifer thought, quickly shrinking away, retreating to the table where she sat down. In seconds, Jake returned and finished off the rest of his lunch although it was nearly cold by now. This time, she didn't asked questions. But her suspicions of Jake were mounting. Who had she really married? Secret phone calls. Mystery cash. Awkward answers. Who was *you-know-who*? She knew she'd have to say something, eventually. But when?

In minutes, they took to the road again, winding their way along Route 66, through the black loam cornfields of Illinois. It was far too cold to put the top down.

Pontiac. . . Bloomington. . . Lincoln. . . Springfield. . .

They rested the night inside the Missouri border at a second-rate hotel on the outskirts of St. Louis. They had covered three hundred miles the first day. Jake made no phone calls and they had a good night's sleep with some love-making mixed in. The second day, they ate breakfast together in a small coffee shop in St. Louis. He bought a newspaper. She bought a new hat, and mailed away a postcard to her parents. Thanks to an early start, they made more ground the second day, over four hundred and fifty miles, through the remainder of the rocky Missouri Ozarks.

Stanton. . . Lebanon. . . Joplin. . .

The eight-cylinder Pierce Arrow ran perfectly for them all the way to Tulsa, Oklahoma. Part-way into the next day, they noticed the countryside was starting to change. The mid-west farmland gave way to the western ranches and oil fields. It was warmer each day and colder each night. It was also less populated. Dry. Dusty in some places. Green in others. Red soil. No pavement. Hardly any trees. Some occasional vehicles. A lot more miles between gas stations and diners.

Stroud. . . Oklahoma City. . . Clinton. . .

By the fourth day, they made it to the Texas Panhandle where the land was laid out flat as a sidewalk and the soil had turned a rich, black loam. Trees were scarce. Grain elevators and oil derricks were plentiful.

Alanreed. . . Amarillo. . . Vega. . .

Then they came upon the rugged terrain and high country of New Mexico.

It was a sunny day with sparse traffic on Route 66. Jennifer had her nose in the business section of the Oklahoma City newspaper they had purchased earlier. She and Jake had thousands invested in two different stocks recommended by her father, money put there by both sides of the family who were avid stock players. Jennifer was her daddy's girl. Her knowledge of the stock market placed her in the minority in most female circles.

"What yuh reading?" he asked, glancing over, as he sped along the road, kicking up red dust behind them.

"The stock pages," she answered. "Just seeing how our nest egg is doing."

"I already know. US Steel up one-half. Browning up by three-quarters."

"Really. . . both up?" she asked. She found the numbers for them. "Yeah."

"You like that?"

"Of course. My father was right. As always. He told us the bull market would continue, even with all the ups and downs of the market these last few weeks."

"Well, he's not always right."

"He's been perfect up to now, Jacob Courtney. You manage to take advantage of his advice."

"Most of the time," Jake admitted.

"He said to put everything we own on US Steel and Browning Manufacturing." She could not hold back any longer. Now was the opportunity. "Jake?"

"Yeah?"

"Who did you talk to on the telephone in Chicago?"

Jake kept his eyes on the road, a rise a hundred yards away. His face twitched. "What the hell is this? I told you before, my dad."

"Did you call your dad at Joliet, too?"

Jake yanked the wheel over to the shoulder and slid to a dusty stop. "How did you know about that?"

Jennifer could see the fire in his eyes. "You took so long in the restroom, so I followed you out."

"You did?"

"Yes, I saw you in the phone booth."

"Spying on me, huh?"

"Why are you looking at me that way? Are you keeping something from me?"

He tried to smile, but it came out a hard frown, almost a sneer. "Did you hear anything?"

"You said, *do it.* And *don't tell you-know-who.* Do what, Jake? Don't tell who?"

"Nothing!" He grabbed onto her sleeve.

She swallowed hard. "Stop it! You're scaring me."

"Jennifer, don't ask me. Not now, anyway."

"Why not now?"

"Please," he said. He reached over and kissed her hard on the mouth. She struggled and pulled away, fixing her hat. "What's the matter with you? Don't try and charm me, Jake Courtney."

He started to grin. "It always worked before."

"Not now it won't."

"Relax, doll."

"Are you in some kind of trouble?"

"Why would you ask that?"

"Something's really weird."

"No, I'm not in trouble. At least, I hope not. Maybe, I don't know."

She put her hand on the door knob. "I don't like this one bit. I'm getting out."

He chuckled. "Sure you are. Right here in no-man's land."

"I am." She opened the door and stepped onto the shoulder. "There. See. I'm out."

"Jennifer!" He shouted through the open passenger door, throwing his hands up. "We're in the middle of nowhere. You get back in here, you silly thing!"

"No! I can't take this anymore. I never could trust you. My daddy said I never should have married you."

"He gave you away, didn't he."

"I think he was drunk at the time."

"He was. But that's beside the point."

"How do I know you're not. . . not some mobster?"

"A mobster whose father owns a department store. Sure, nice try."

She slammed the door and strutted away into the western sun. He jumped out and stood by the front bumper. He calmly lit a cigarette. "Can't go too far without a suitcase. Nearest town is Albuquerque, fifteen miles *behind us.*"

"I don't care." She kept walking, her back to him, her hat in her hand.

"You spoiled little brat. It's getting chilly and it'll be dark in a few hours. You don't even have a coat. You'll freeze." No response from her. "All right then. Goodbye!" He got back in the car, put the vehicle in gear and began driving away, slowly, passing his wife, and leaving her behind in a cloud of dust. He remembered his father telling him once that there were two theories to arguing with a woman. Trouble was, neither one worked.

Suddenly realizing that Jake meant business, she began to run after him. But it was no use. He sped up and drove out of sight over the rise. She stopped and dusted herself off. Jake was right. It *was* getting cold. She began to cry. When she got to the top of the hill and looked down, there was the Pierce Arrow pulled over by the shoulder. Jennifer ran for it and into the arms of her husband waiting at the back bumper. She smothered him with kisses.

"Don't leave me. Please don't leave me," she gasped.

"On one condition."

"What's that?"

"Don't ask me anymore questions, OK?"

"I won't. I promise."

"I'll explain in due time."

His voice soothed her. "All right. Just don't leave me. I'm not a spoiled brat, am I?"

He shrugged. "Just sometimes." He opened his door, cigarette in his mouth. "Wait. I have to go."

"You mean. . . *go*?"

"Yeah. Really bad."

"Now?" she asked. "Here?"

"Yeah, here. Where else? In the car? Don't watch now," he grinned.

"Don't worry. I won't."

Two hours later, they bedded down at a motel in Laguna for the night, where they were too tired to do anything but sleep.

Day five, they drove the rest of the way through northern New Mexico and into Arizona. They were making good time. They stayed on Route 66 and took a detour north at Williams to see the Grand Canyon, one of the eight wonders of the world. The couple savored the sight on the rail at one of the south rim points with a dozen other sightseers. More colors than one could comprehend.

"Amazing," Jennifer said.

Jake's eyes grew wide. "I second that."

"Kind of cold."

"You bet it is."

"Hold me."

"With pleasure."

The morning of October 29 broke as most mornings did that time of year in Arizona. The sun was shining bright. No wind. Day six on the Route 66 trail west for the couple as they left their Williams hotel.

Seligman... Kingman... Oatman... Topack...

This was dry country. Fatigue was setting in now. It was a hot day, close to one hundred degrees. They reached the Arizona-California state line by evening, only minutes before the sunset. They crossed over the Colorado River, got out of the grimy Pierce Arrow and stood before the sign stating WELCOME TO CALIFORNIA.

Both were silent for a long time.

"We did it," Jake said.

Jennifer agreed, nodding. "Yeah. Good thing. We're starting to run out of clean clothes."

The Courtneys held each other. Up the road, they saw the sign for Needles... *ten miles*. This part of California appeared bleak. Behind them were the Black Mountains of Arizona and the scariest driving they had ever experienced. The mountain passes had been murder on the nerves. Open desert ahead for a hundred miles after Needles, they were told at their last Arizona stop before the wicked descent that they had finished.

They drove into Needles, an oasis town of a few thousand, where Jake steered the Pierce Arrow into a Mobil gas station.

"Fill it up," he said to the teenage male attendant dressed all in white.

"Clean the windshield?"

"Yeah, it sure needs it," Jake replied.

Jennifer glanced over at the open door to the business. Inside were three old men in their fifties or sixties listening intently to a large cabinet radio in the corner. One of the men shook his head. All three were silent. She rolled her own window down. The radio was certainly loud enough. Something about the New York Stock Market. "Jake?" she said, glancing at her husband.

"What?"

"Over there."

He looked to where she pointed. "Yeah, so?"

She emerged from the car and walked slowly towards the men, listening as she went. She stopped at the doorway. "Hello, there."

"Good evening, ma'am," one of the men replied.

All three stood up for her.

"Please sit down. May I ask what you're listening to?"

Jake followed up behind her.

"The news."

"Aren't you a long ways from any radio station out here?"

"It's a Los Angeles station, ma'am. It starts coming in real clear across the desert this time of day."

She nodded at the large cabinet. "What exactly are you listening to?"

"Stock Market reports. All hell seems to be breaking loose out there in New York City."

She listened to the announcer for a moment. Stock prices were announced on the air, all of them down. "What is it all about?"

"The New York Stock Market crashed, ma'am. Everything's down."

"It didn't crash," another man said. "It blew up. Worst day in her history."

Jennifer's throat tightened. "Oh, my God!" Her eyes sought her husband.

She came to, and looked around, groggy. "What happened?"

Jake was slumped over in the front seat of the Pierce Arrow, holding her. "Relax, doll. Yuh fainted."

"I never fainted before in my life." She felt her head. "How long was I out for?"

"Three or four minutes, at least."

She bolted upright. "Ouch! My head's sore."

"Easy. You banged it on the door frame when you fell."

"The news? Is it true?"

"Yep, 'fraid so. The Stock Market really did crash all right."

She was annoyed that Jake, for some reason, didn't appear as disturbed as her by the news. "We're broke, Jake. Our families. All of us."

"What do you mean?"

"Before we left New York, my father told me that he convinced your father to invest everything he had this week in Browning and US Steel. He even remortgaged his house. They both did. He was so. . . so sure."

"Some hot tip, huh?"

She closed her eyes. "Jake! We're finished."

"Look, doll, we don't have all the details. When we reach Los Angeles, we'll read what the papers have to say. I'll call New York, too."

Jennifer frowned. "If you can get through."

One of the men in the station walked towards them. "Is your wife OK?" he asked, politely.

"Fine, thanks," Jake replied.

Jennifer sighed. "Yes, thank you."

"Where yuh headed?"

"Los Angeles," Jake replied.

"That right? Where yuh from?"

"New York."

"Yuh drove all the way, did yuh?"

"From Chicago we did."

"Good fer you. A lot of people are doing that now with this new road. And there's going to be more coming."

"So I've heard."

The man rubbed his chin. "Mind if I give you some advice?"

"Not at all."

"Please do," Jennifer said.

"You got a few hundred miles of Mojave desert ahead of yuh. She's still pretty hot during the day, even in October. Go through it at night, when it's much cooler. Especially this time of year."

Jake looked grateful. "Really?"

The man nodded. "Yep. And take some water with yuh. Ice, if you can. Make sure the gas tank and rad are topped up, too. I can help you out with everything you need."

"Thanks."

"Hungry?"

"Sort of."

"Come on. I'll fix you up there, too."

In Los Angeles the next day, the Courtneys woke early and received the full facts from newspaper accounts in the spacious hotel lobby. The crash had been devastating. Over 16 million shares were sold in one day, amounting to billions of dollars. Millions of people lost every cent they owned. Suicides were reported. People shot themselves in back alleys and their homes. Others jumped from Wall Street office windows. The Courtneys had read enough of the gloom and left for morning coffee and toast in the dining room, although neither were that hungry.

"I'll be right back," Jake said, settling her into a chair.

"Where yuh going now?" she asked.

He smirked. "I'm gonna phone New York."

He returned almost thirty minutes later, which seemed like eternity to Jennifer, who was now in tears.

"Doll," Jake began, "I have to tell you something. The good news first."

"What?" she sniffed, her face down.

"We didn't lose a cent."

As if by magic, the tears stopped. She looked up. "What, what do you mean?"

"I told you before I'd explain." He lit a cigarette, exhaled noisily, and began. "The phone calls in Chicago and Joliet were to my pop. I advised him to sell all his shares, *everything*, immediately. Two days earlier I told someone in your father's firm to sell our stocks. I didn't tell your father. He wasn't supposed to know."

She wiped her eyes with her hand. "You sold everything?"

"That's right, doll."

"Did your father do the same?"

"It took the second phone call to finally convince him. By the way, he never did remortgage his house."

"My father was the *you-know-who*, wasn't he?"

"Yes. I thought it best to go through someone else. Just in case he would try to talk me out of it."

"So, was there really a savings account?"

He shook his head. "Nope. Cashed in my stocks and got my dad to wire me the money for the car and other expenses."

"Yeah? But what were you so nervous about?"

"I was going on a hunch," he admitted. "I had a premonition or something. I don't know. I just couldn't explain it. I had to wait to see if my hunch was right. I couldn't tell your father. He was so struck on us keeping the stocks."

"So, how much money do we have?"

He perked up. "We made some money when the prices shot up that one big day at the beginning of the week."

"How much?"

"After paying cash for the car and expenses along the way. . ."

"Oh, for heaven's sake! How much, Jake?"

"We still have over twenty thousand dollars. And it's all tucked safely away where we can get at it."

"Jake, I could kiss you." She did.

"Wait a minute! What about my father? My mother? I wonder how they're doing?"

Jake rubbed his face. He couldn't put it off. "Well. . ."

"What's the matter? Are my parents all right?"

"That's the bad news. Your father must have convinced a few others to invest."

"Why do you say that?" She cleared her throat. "Jake, you know something? What is it?"

Her husband held her hand, gently. "Hold onto your hat, baby. It must have been hard for him to deal with."

"What was? What is it, Jake?"

"Well. . . you see. . . he committed suicide. He shot himself."

"What!"

He swallowed hard. "And he shot your mother, too."

Jennifer fainted for the second time in her life.

SANTA MONICA, CALIFORNIA

This was the end of the line for the Route 66 adventure that had suddenly gone sour. Here they were at the Santa Monica beach, the blue waters of the Pacific Ocean only a few feet away. Jennifer—in a daze—and Jake strolled the beach sands, eventually sitting on a wooden pier to talk, as the golden sun set slowly, grandly over the calm water.

"I have a great idea, doll." He was holding her hand. "I love it here in California. Warm weather. Sunshine. Palm trees. It's a tonic, especially after what's happened."

"I like it, too," she said between tears, her parents still on her mind.

"I know what we can do with the money."

"Must we talk about it now. We should go back to New York and see my sister. She must be devastated."

"I think we *should* talk about it. Listen, let's move here and open a hotel business. You and me, together."

She nearly collapsed. "A hotel! What brought this on!"

"A small place, where we can afford the down payment. We can borrow the rest."

She pulled her hands away. "A hotel?"

"Yep."

"Where?"

"I was thinking the other side of San Bernardino. This side of the desert."

"We don't know anything about running a hotel."

"So?"

"So!"

"Did Edison know anything about the light bulb before he discovered it? Never mind that. OK. Bad example. Look, with all the Route 66 traffic back and forth these next few years, it would be a perfect spot. Get the road travelers going out and the ones coming back in. Just far enough away from Los Angeles to bed down, have some food. Sell lots of fresh orange juice from the orchards. We could make ourselves a pile of dough."

"What's your father going to say? He has a job waiting for you. A good one. He'll think you lost your marbles."

"Leave him to me."

Jennifer shook her head. "Oh. . . Jake. Everything is just happening too fast."

"We'll go back to New York, all right. See your family. Pay our respects. Besides, all our belongings are there. But we're *moving here*. Got it, doll? We're moving here. Let's start new."

She heaved a sigh. "Jake. . ."

"It'll be good for us. You'll see."

And so their second adventure began.

2

Man in Black

The Stock Market Crash of 1929 ushered in the Great Depression. By the early 1930s banks failed, factories closed their doors, millions were out of work. Desperate men sold apples and pencils on street corners. Then, to make matters worse, a drought covered the mid-west. Oklahoma was one of the hardest hit areas. Route 66 quickly became the road of flight. In the extreme northeast corner of the state—a rifle shot off Route 66 and less than ten miles from both the Kansas and the Missouri borders—sat the town of Quapaw, known locally for one thing. They called it Spooklight, a common but unexplainable flash of bright light that bounced and bobbed near Devil's Promenade, a bluff a mile north of town.

NEAR PRESENT-DAY QUAPAW, OKLAHOMA—SPRING, 1874

Six dusty and hardened men rode over the Missouri border into Oklahoma Territory. In a clearing surrounded by bushes and rock, they dismounted to give their horses a much-needed rest.

"What do yuh think, Tom?" one of them said.

The leader of the tired group walked ahead of the others to the edge of the cliff and looked up to the top. Going by the alias of Tom Howard, he insisted that they all use aliases whenever they could, even within the privacy of the gang. It was a good way to get used to the habit.

Howard eyed the land at the base of the bluff and finally said, "We camp here for the night."

"Sure thing, Tom," one of the riders said. The others agreed with nods. They had to stop some time. They had been in the saddle all day to keep ahead of any posses that may have dared to chase after them, never expecting anyone to follow them this far.

As the sun began to set, Howard scratched his red-brown moustache, his icy eyes moving over the lay of the land. This was a perfect spot. He could see for miles in three directions. He recalled with satisfaction the Missouri Pacific Railroad train they had robbed three days before at a small station in Taney County, Missouri, where they came away $12,000 richer. It was almost too easy. All they did was pile up some rocks on the tracks and when the westbound train hissed and screeched to a stop, they jumped out and ordered the safe opened at gun point. They also helped themselves to any cash or jewels in the possession of the frightened passengers.

Howard was in the "Robbery Business." It provided a good living, as well as a profitable one. And he was cold blooded about it. A callous killer, he feared no man. Anybody who got in his way would be taken care of, just like one fancy-dressed man back on the train who tried to be a hero by grabbing a gang member's gun. Howard shot him dead with his smoking Colt Navy revolver. Howard was proud of his profession, too. He enjoyed reading about his "exploits" in such papers as the *St. Louis Dispatch* and the *Kansas City Times*. He often would write the editors after his robberies to confirm whether it was his gang that engaged in a particular act of thievery, knowing full well that there were those bandits out there who tried to imitate him and take the credit for something that wasn't rightfully theirs.

Howard sat on a large rock and removed a piece of paper from his coat pocket. With the sun hiding now behind the horizon, he wanted to pencil a few notes on the sheet before it would get too dark. While he contemplated his next move, he glanced over at the five members of the gang, and thought he saw a flick of light off to the side.

"What was that?" someone said.

"I don't know." Howard turned, jerking his head back and forth. He drew his revolver and squatted, the paper clutched in his hand. In an instant, the others did the same, their eyes west. "I don't see anything now."

"Me, neither. Think it was a lantern?"

"Could be, I reckon," Howard replied.

"Maybe they know we're over here."

"I dunno," Howard replied. "I don't think it's a posse. Not from that direction. I don't a-reckon they had time to come right around us."

"There it is again," someone said. "Coming this a-way."

The gang had their guns at ready. They waited. Nothing. Howard stood. It was nearly dark now.

"Where did it go?"

"I don't know," Howard answered.

Then, there it was, behind them, only thirty feet or so above them, against the cliff. It was a bright, white-blue glow, several feet in diameter, racing haphazardly up the solid rock. No sound. It was so bright that the men had to squint their eyes. One man fired at it. It was no use. Now it was coming down the cliff even faster. *Closer. Closer*

"What is that?" Howard exclaimed.

Then it kept speeding towards them... *so fast... so bright...* until it went right past the spot where Howard was standing.

Howard groaned... and dropped to his knees as if punched in the ribs.

CHEROKEE, KANSAS—SUMMER, 1935

Rufus Elder hoped and prayed that his beat-up, dented 1926 Ford truck would make it. Mildred, as he called the crate, had a lot of miles on her. Maybe too many for a trip like this. The original black paint job was peeling badly. The tire treads were worn. The windshield had two distinct cracks. The oil pan was leaking. The rad would often overheat, even on short runs. Nonetheless, Rufus, along with his plump wife, Jackie, and skinny, dirty-faced boys, Willie and Jody, ages five and six, were determined to reach California and start all over again, against all odds. A better life, hopefully. Why not? Rufus and Jackie were still young, under thirty-five, although the harsh farm life had aged them these last few years. The family had no choice but to pack up. They were broke. No crops. Dying cattle. Little food. Only the grubby clothes on their backs and a few precious belongings.

The Elders were honest and good folk. Farming stock, three generations back. But they had to think of the future. What about their sons? And their grandkids? They needed an education, if that was possible. There was nothing much to draw from in Kansas. Farming couldn't cut it. Some families had already left. Others had died of the fever. Rufus and Jackie were the first of their kin to cut loose, despite what they were hearing about the border patrols at the California state line, vigilantes with shovels and two-by-fours preventing outsiders from entering the state.

It was hot the evening that the Elders left the farm for good. The family of four crammed into the bench seat of the Ford truck heading south for the Route 66 hookup in Oklahoma that would lead them all the way west to the Promised Land. It took them most of the day to pack. Mattresses. Box springs. A desk. Chairs. A washtub. Shovels. A garbage can. Wood crates with knick-knacks. Then, they were on their way. The wind was up. The first thing Rufus thought of was that another "duster" was gaining momentum from out of the west, those dreaded things that would blow the topsoil across the country. It was unusual for the wind to be up at this time of the evening.

As Rufus drove along at thirty miles per hour—the truck heavy laden with all the belongings his family could take—his eyes were rooted to the western horizon. To his relief, the wind seemed to be dying off. No duster today, he hoped. Who needed another damn one of those things. He remembered one real bad duster that spring that had darkened the sky for days and was told that it had covered clean across Texas and all the way to Kansas. For days, Rufus had done everything he could think of to keep the dust away, including jamming newspapers under doors and windows. Outside, he and his family wetted bits of clothes and wrapped them around there faces. Schools and businesses closed. No one drove anywhere. People choked to death. Livestock died of thirst. Rufus never wished he and his family to go through that again. No sir. California here they come. Regardless of the border patrols, which was probably the least of their worries.

The truck lumbered over the dirt road towards the state line, the towns of Roseland, Columbus and Riverton disappearing behind them. All around them the scenery resembled a trip to the moon. Sand and gray dirt. No topsoil left. Dry as a bone baked in an oven. An hour after leaving the farm, Rufus and Jackie saw the road sign welcoming them to a new state.

"Look, boys, it's Oklahoma," Jackie said, pointing through the windshield.

Rufus puffed on his pipe, content. The sun was setting over the land. He put the headlights on. They had made it this far without the radiator overheating. Mind you, he was keeping the speed down. Then his whiskered face frowned when it gripped him. Good Lord in heaven, they had seventeen hundred miles to go! He didn't want to think about it. *Just point the nose, fellah. . . and drive.*

"What's the matter, Rufe?" Jackie asked, the youngest boy, Willie, in her lap.

"Oh, nothing."

"We're going to make it, aren't we?"

Rufus rubbed the three-day growth on his face. "Yeah, you bet we will," he confirmed.

She smiled. She was a good woman, hardly ever in a bad mood. "I'm busting a gut to see California."

"Me, too."

"Me, too, ma," Willie said.

"They say you pick fresh fruit for breakfast."

Rufus nodded at his wife. "That's right, mama. Peaches, oranges, you name 'er. So they say."

He took another dirt road west then south towards Quapaw. After several minutes, he braked the truck near a cliff, off from the road. He was lost and hoped to get his bearings in the twilight. He stepped from the truck, letting the truck run with the lights on.

"There's a town over yonder, Rufe. See the lights?"

"Yeah. Should be Quapaw."

"I can see the road, too."

"That's 'er, mama. Route 66. We're here."

Rufus and Jackie hugged, as Rufus shut the engine off.

Suddenly, a light flashed behind them. At first they thought it was the headlights of another car only a few feet away. But they quickly changed their minds when the light circled them before disappearing up the cliff.

"What's that, Rufe?"

Rufus stood, unable to move. "Well, I'll be jiggered. So, it is true."

"What's true?"

"Spooklight. The stories are true."

"Spooklight? What are you talking about?"

"Here it comes again, ma."

25

The light now came streaking down the cliff at a tremendous speed. Then they felt the eerie presence of a harsh wind followed by a bright, static explosion that shook the ground and threw all four Elders backwards. When the light finally vanished a few moments later, they found a man in dark clothing lying in the dirt, a revolver in the palm of his hand.

"Where did he come from?" Jackie asked, rubbing her eyes, as if she were caught in a dream.

"I don't know." Rufus found his lantern in the back of the truck and lit it with a match. "Let me see here."

"Is he dead?"

"I don't know that either."

The Elders drew closer to the man on the ground. Over him now, Rufus bent down for a closer look, setting the lantern on the ground. His eyes jumped to the gun in his hand. "If that don't beat all, mama."

"What?"

"The gun. Look at 'er. That's got to be as old as the hills. That's a Colt Navy revolver. My great-grandpappy had himself one of those in the Civil War. What do you suppose—"

"Look, pa," Jody said, running up to a crumpled piece of paper on the ground. He ran it back to his father.

"Let's see it, boy."

"What is it, Rufe?"

The man in black began to stir.

"He's alive, pa," Jody said, clutching his mother's skirt.

The man on the ground shielded his eyes from the bright lantern with his hand.

"You OK, mister?" Rufus asked with sympathy, squatting over the man.

Tom Howard jerked awake, and leaned on one elbow. Groggy, he felt for his gun, pointing it at the images in the night. "Jeb, that you? *Jeb?*"

"Easy. Nobody named Jeb, here, mister. My name is Rufus Elder and this here is my wife, Jackie, and my boys—"

"Where did you come from?" Howard asked nervously, crawling, then groping to his feet.

"We were gonna ask you the same question. You can put that there gun down now. We ain't gonna hurt yuh."

"What are you doing here?"

"Just traveling through, mister. Going to California. How about you?"

Howard pointed the barrel at the truck. "What's that thing?"

"What's what?"

"That!" Howard shouted.

Rufus frowned. "You mean the truck?"

"What is it?"

"You're acting awfully strange, mister. Ain't you never seen a truck before?"

"Where are the horses?"

"It. . . it doesn't have any horses."

"What is this place?"

"Oklahoma. That is Quapaw over there, yonder."

"Who else is with yuh?" Howard asked, clearing his throat.

"No one. Just us four."

"Where are my boys?"

"Who?"

"The others. . . who were here?"

"We didn't see anybody, mister."

"You didn't?"

"No, sir. Only you."

"What did you do with them?"

"I told yuh we didn't see anybody."

"Did you see the light? The bright light!"

"You mean the flash? Yeah, we sure did see it. The ground shook and there you were."

Howard's eyes grew wide. Staring off, he said, "The last thing I remember was I saw the light and. . . I woke up. Now. . . now you're here." He rubbed his face with his hand. He gulped. "This is not possible. Those lights out there. Who's out there?"

"Where?"

"There." Howard pointed off in the distance.

"Like I said, mister, that's the town of Quapaw."

"I don't remember no town round here."

"It's been there for some time, mister. A few hundred people."

Howard put his hand on his forehead and groaned.

"You don't look well, mister. Can we help?"

Howard stepped back. "No. Stay where you are."

27

"Put the gun away, please. Like I said, we won't hurt yuh." Rufus looked over at his wife beside him. The sons moved in closer to their parents. "Look, mister, we best be on our way."

"You're not going anywhere!" Howard aimed his gun directly at Rufus's head. "You're staying right here until my boys return!"

"We can't do that. You see—"

Howard cocked the pistol, a clear crack of sound in the night. "Shut up! You're staying here."

Rufus put his arm around his wife. "You say so, mister."

"What's that in your hand?"

"This?" Rufus said, holding his arm out straight. "It's a piece of paper we found on the ground."

"Give it to me. Now!"

"Sure thing, mister."

Howard stepped forward and snatched it from Rufus's hand.

"What yuh so edgy about, mister? And where did yuh get that gun? She's a Colt Navy revolver. That's a relic. My great-grandpappy had one of those in the Civil War."

"Shut up!" Howard screamed, stuffing the paper inside his coat pocket.

"Why do you keep telling us to shut up, mister."

"I said, shut up! I have to think!"

QUAPAW—SPRING, 1874

"Where'd yer brother go, Jeb?"

The man called Jeb was just as confused as the others. "Hell if I know."

It was pitch dark now. The moon was at half glow. The temperature was dropping by the minute.

"What was that bright light? Ain't never seen anything like that before. One second Tom was here and the next he was gone. Look around. He's gotta be here."

"Right."

Jeb stood on the exact piece of ground where he had last seen his brother. He glanced up the cliff. *Where had he gone to. . . and so damn fast?*

QUAPAW—SUMMER, 1935

Howard sauntered over to the truck, his gun aimed on the family of four. Curious, he saw steam rising from the radiator, and placed his free hand on the cap.

"Ouch!" He jumped back. "What the hell is that!"

"Watch it, mister. Don't you know you're not supposed to touch a hot rad?"

"A what?" Howard wiggled his hand.

"A hot rad." Rufus shook his head. "What yuh expect? The engine's been running all day."

Howard walked around the front of the truck, ending up at the passenger side. He banged the door with his fist. Metal. "No horses, eh?"

"No, sir."

"What's all this in the back of 'er? Going somewhere?"

"Yes, sir. Like I said, California."

"All the way to California! You crazy!"

"She'll make it."

Howard felt the cracked windshield. "Glass," he said, "jess like a window."

"That's right, mister."

Howard raised the gun and hit a section of the windshield with the barrel. The glass was tougher than he thought. Nothing like a house window. He smashed it harder this time, poking a two-inch hole through it.

"Hey, wait a minute, here!" Rufus shouted, rushing towards the man.

Howard fired off the two pistol shots at Rufus's feet. "Don't try anything. Or you'll be in a messa trouble."

Rufus backed off.

Howard rubbed his hand over the front passenger tire, noticing the rubber. "What this?"

Jackie turned to her husband. "He scares me, Rufe," she whispered.

"Me, too," he whispered back.

"I said, what's this!"

"It's a rubber tire."

"Why isn't it made of wood, like other wagons?"

Rufus shook his head. He was losing his patience. "I don't know."

Howard fired another shot, this time directly at the tire, and watched it go flat. Rufe had had enough. He charged Howard, tackling him to the ground. Howard's hat flew off, his pistol flinging several feet away.

29

He broke free and scrambled for the gun. Rufus tackled him again, then pinned him to the ground. Howard punched Rufus in the ribs, jumped to his feet, and retrieved the gun.

"Enough of that! All of you, sit down over by that. . . thing. Yonder. That horseless buggy. Now!"

Rufus and his family moved over to the truck. Jackie held her husband. "Are you all right, Rufe?" she asked, looking into his face.

"Yeah, I'm OK," he grunted, staring hard at the man in black.

"Let's make ourselves all nice and comfortable." Keeping his eye on the family, Howard grabbed the lantern and took it over to the large rock that he had sat on when his gang were still around. He waited. Fifteen minutes passed. He finally pulled out his piece of paper and the pencil, and started writing. Then, out of the corner of his eye, he saw it. A flash! Up the cliff.

"There it is again, pa. The light," Willie said.

"Yeah, so it is."

Howard rose to his feet, his attention on the light. All five transfixed, they watched as the light bobbed to the left. . . to the right. . . steadily moving down the cliff.

"She's coming this way, mister."

Howard was too mesmerized to move. The light raced down the cliff, bobbing, weaving. . . left, right. . . then whisked by the five of them. They all felt the breeze. It was more gold in color than before, and brighter. It was much larger, too. Ten feet wide, ten feet high. Off it went over a rise. . . then, in an instant, it came back. *Right for them. Brighter. . . brighter. . .*

They all felt the static explosion.

QUAPAW—SPRING, 1874

Jeb was the first to come to. Sitting up, he glanced around. The bright light was gone. Nowhere to be seen. What force. Twice in less than an hour and it had knocked them out both times.

"Hey! Hey you guys!"

Others began to wake.

"What the hell is that thing?" one of them said.

Jeb leaned over and *there he was.* "Tom. Hey, looka here. It's Tom!"

Tom Howard opened his eyes and saw the silhouettes of several men standing over him.

"Tom? Where yuh been?"

Howard lay still. "Jeb?"

"Yeah, it's me. Where in tarnation have you been?"

"I was going to ask you guys the same question."

"We were right here all the time." Jeb helped his brother to his feet. "This is crazy."

"Did you see the light again?"

"Yeah, we saw it."

Howard looked around. "Did you see the buggy?"

"What buggy?"

"The metal one without the horses. The truck, they called 'er."

"Truck? You must've got one real good bump on yer head."

"No, I saw it. Honest. A man and a woman were standing beside it. They had two boys. Steam coming from 'er. They said it had something called tires. They were going to California."

"Come on, Tom," another member said. "There's no-one around here for miles but us."

Howard grunted. "I saw them, I tell you. I saw them!"

"Sure you did," Jeb said. "You were dreaming. Must've happened when yuh got knocked out."

Howard stumbled over to where he last saw the buggy. He got on his knees. "I smashed the glass! It was thick. Real thick!"

Jeb walked over with him. "What glass?"

"Put a hole clean through 'er. She was right here, I tell you. Right here."

"Tom, get up. Quit joshing us."

"The wheels weren't wood. The fellow called it a tire. A rubber tire."

"You said that already."

Howard looked up at his brother and the others crowding around. "They were here. Then the light came back. The flash. And I was back with you guys." He rubbed his face. No one spoke until he flung his arms out and said, "Let's get the hell out of here."

"But I thought you wanted us to make camp."

"Not here. This place has a curse or something on it. Not here. Let's ride."

Jeb shrugged. "You say so, Tom."

"Come on." Howard stood. "Where's my horse?"

Jeb smirked. "Right where yuh left it, Tom. By the rock."

Rufus elder changed the truck's flat by the light of the lantern. His wife and boys sat nearby, as he explained what he knew of the local story.

"They call 'er Spooklight," he grunted, raising the side of Mildred up with his tire jack. "My grandpappy told me about it. Gosh, ma, it's a good thing I brought along a spare. Didn't think I'd need to use 'er so soon, though."

"What is a Spooklight, pa?" Willie asked, wide-eyed.

"No one seems to know, boy. Grandpappy told me it's been around since the Quapaw Indian days. Balls of fire and light. They move around... come and go."

"Pa?" Willie asked a second question. "Who was that man and where'd he go?"

Rufus was removing the shot-up tire now. "I don't know and I don't care. Good riddance to him. I don't ever want to see him again."

"Pa?"

"*Yes, Jody?*" Rufus huffed, annoyed, as he sweated with the wrench on the tire bolts.

"What's this?" he said, handing his father a sheet of crumpled paper.

Jackie came closer. "That's the paper the man had."

Rufus grabbed the sheet. "Bring that lantern over here, Jody."

"Sure, pa."

Rufus opened the sheet up and read it.

"She's a wanted poster. *Jesse James.*" He felt his throat going dry. "A ten thousand dollar reward for his capture. Goes by the alias of Tom Howard."

"That looks like the man, pa," Jody said, excited. "That's him."

Rufus crushed the paper in his fist. "No, it's not."

"That sure does look like him, Rufe."

"It's not him, ma. Let me fix this flat so that we can get out of here. This is screwy. Screwy, I tell you."

"Wait a second." Jackie opened her husband's hand and removed the piece of paper. "There's something else on it. "Remember, he was writing in pencil."

"Yeah, I remember."

"Says here, let's see," she said, moving closer to the light, and unraveling it. "Says here... *Dear Kansas City Times Editor. We had nothing*

to do with the bank robbery at Joplin in June. Yours truly, Jesse James.
What do you think, Rufe?"

"Let me jess fix this tire so we can high-tail it outta here, woman."

Twenty minutes later, Rufus had the flat fixed and the family boarded Mildred. Glad to be behind the wheel once again, he motored onto Route 66.

Rufus glanced over at his wife. The boys were sleeping, both leaning against their mother. He pressed the accelerator and the truck picked up speed in the night, the headlights reflecting off a Route 66 road sign that quickly came and went.

"Grandpappy always said that strange things happened on the nights when Spooklight was out and about," he said.

All Jackie could do was nod in agreement as she looked west through the damaged windshield, around the hole left from the man's Navy Colt revolver.

3

The Hostess with the Mostess

While Adolf Hitler's armies were marching across Europe in 1941, Route 66 was evolving. As the road improved—paved fully by 1938—and saw more traffic, the gas station restrooms along the way became more used. The more they were used, the filthier they became. Complaints soon came pouring in, mostly from women travelers. One gas company in particular decided that something had to be done. In 1939, the Phillips 66 company hired registered nurses—called Highway Hostesses—to clean up. They were first sent on a course, then hit the road, up and down the highways inspecting restrooms with the "white-glove test."

The plan was to drop in on each station at least once a month. Phillips 66 stations were going to be "the best, the cleanest restrooms in the nation." The nurses were also expected to help distressed motorists in need. Each nurse's back seat and trunk held a first-aid kit, Lysol, and a mechanic's tool box, which they also knew how to use. This is the story of one such Highway Hostess nurse who had a trip she would never forget.

Outside Springfield, Missouri—September, 1941

She steered her cream-colored 1940 Plymouth sedan onto the gravel shoulder behind the Buick convertible, where a young man was bent over the hood. The top was down, the hood was up. It was a warm afternoon, near six o'clock. The man's shirt sleeves were pushed up to his elbows. As her training had dictated, she got out, went around to the back bumper of her car, opened the trunk and reached for her metal toolbox. If the fellah was going to try something, at least she had a weapon or two.

He straightened up and gawked at her. About twenty-five, he unbuttoned the top button on his shirt and loosened his tie. She could tell he was a handsome specimen of a man with black, curly, well-oiled hair. Following the direction of his eyes, she could almost read his every thought. He was noting the Phillips 66 logo on the driver door and the printed words CERTIFIED REST ROOMS along with her name, BETTY MCDOUGALD, R.N. He also saw the orange-and-black Phillips 66 patch on her coat. The last thing he probably expected was a tall, attractive thirty-year old strawberry blonde in a matching soft-blue cap, waistcoat, skirt, and white blouse, carrying a tool box. She knew how he felt. It just didn't fit. A liberated company girl driving a company car. Out, all by herself.

"Trouble?" Betty asked, pushing her hand through her hair.

"Yeah. You bet."

"Can't get it started?"

"You're right." The young man was still in shock at the sight of her coming to his rescue. Men were supposed to do this for women. Not the other way around. "I pulled over for a few winks. But when I woke up and I hit the ignition, no go."

"Any sound? A click. . . a spark?"

"Nothing."

"I see."

"Do you know something about cars?" he finally asked.

"Nothing," she replied, with a self-assured smirk. "That's why I carry this tool box around with me."

He backed off. "OK."

Betty walked around the side of the car, setting her toolkit down. "Hmm. Straight eight. Lots of power."

"You're right about that."

"Kind of greasy, though. You should keep better care of it." She wiggled the battery cables one at a time. One was loose. She flipped the lid up on the toolbox, grabbed the appropriate wrench and tightened the cable. "There. Try it now," she said, wiping her hands on a rag.

"Sure thing."

As soon as he got behind the wheel and turned the ignition, the long straight-eight started. He revved it a few times, and she clanged the hood closed.

They were both smiling.

"Thanks," he said, gratefully, shutting the motor off.

"Don't mention it. I do it all the time. Hostess McDougald to the rescue."

"You're no deadbeat with a toolbox, that's for sure." He held out his hand and she shook it. "I'm Tony."

"I'm Betty."

"Hi, Betty."

"Where yuh headed?"

"Oklahoma City." He lit a cigarette.

"You look thirsty," she said. "I have a cooler full of ice in the back seat. Most of it's melted down by now. I know it's far from a cold beer, but you want a drink?"

"Sure," he said, exhaling a cloud of smoke. "Sounds great."

Soon, they were drinking ice water from paper cups, leaning against the convertible. Betty seemed to enjoy herself, her first long, friendly conversation with a man for weeks, outside of her work. To their surprise, they were both from St. Louis. Tony said he was an insurance salesman out of a job, but hoping to get another such position soon. She had tried various jobs, like clerking and waitressing, then she enrolled in a nurse's course in Tulsa, Oklahoma. After graduating, the Phillips 66 Petroleum Company in Bartlesville, Oklahoma hired her. Starting something new can be good for you, she advised him. Maybe he should try it.

"So, how'd yuh nab a job like this, traveling around the country?" he asked, toying with his cup in his hand.

"Oh," she shrugged, "lucky, I guess. My girl friend in Joplin saw an ad in the paper. I got it. Here I am."

"Do you like it?"

"It's OK. Company car and all."

"So, you're a card-carrying nurse, are yuh? An RN?"

"Yes, sir."

"Well, you do one fine job. Yuh sure helped me out."

"Thank you."

"How long you been doing this?"

"Two weeks," she admitted.

"Is that all? Aren't you concerned about your safety? You know, a girl on the road all the time, by herself. "

"Don't you worry. I can take care of myself."

He nodded, slowly, convinced. "I bet you can. What does your husband think about it all?"

"He doesn't know. I haven't seen him for two years."

"Oh. . . sorry."

"Don't be. I'm not. He ran out on me."

"On your own ever since, eh?"

"That's right."

He threw the empty cup in his back seat. "Well, I best be going. Thanks for the cool one. Nice talking to yuh, Betty."

"Same here. By the way," she said, "quit smoking. It's bad for you."

"Says who?"

"Medical reports."

"Ah, you nurses," he kidded her, opening the car door to slide behind the wheel. As he pulled away, he waved in the rear-view mirror.

She waved back.

She stood there for a few moments. Tony wasn't such a bad fellow. She was glad that he didn't try anything. A nice, polite young man. But kind of a hotshot and a little too young for her, though.

Betty headed in the same direction, but turned off the road towards the first motel she saw less than ten miles away, an establishment that had a dozen separate cabins, and a coffee shop, all in art deco. She glanced around. She was tired after a full day. The Breezeway Court had tiled walls, glass-block windows, and flat roofs. The postcard she removed from the glove box full of other postcards told her that the place had air-conditioned units, reasonable rates, and that inspections were invited.

She looked up.

A few cars were parked on the gravel off to the right near the large flagpole where the Stars and Stripes was flying. There were vacancies, according to the flashy, fifteen-foot-high, orange-and-white neon sign. She hoped the room was cleaner than the motel she had slept in the night before, the one that had mildew growing in the shower and the two mouse traps under the bed. If this one wasn't up to standard, she wouldn't stay. Period. Not this time. Not with Springfield only thirty minutes away, where a decent pick of overnight accommodations were probably available all over town. She returned the postcard to the stack of others in the glove box and flipped the door closed.

Head high, she strutted into the office, where a white-haired desk clerk about sixty stirred from his chair behind the counter.

He smiled. "Hello, there."

"Hello, yourself," she smiled back.

"Looking for a room, young lady?" he asked.

"Yes. But I'd like to see it first."

"I don't mind." He reached behind him to the pine rack on the wall to remove a key. "There you go, ma'am. Cabin number three. Around the corner on the left."

"Thank you. Be right back."

"I'll be here."

She took the key in hand, found the cabin, and unlocked the door. Inside, a quick look around, she saw that it was a neat, tan-colored room in a pastel tone with white shades. Queen size bed, neatly folded sheets. The two windows were closed, but it was still cool, despite the day's heat. Air-conditioner in the window. No musty smell. In the bathroom, she threw back the curtain and peeked in at the shower. The tiles sparkled. Shiny enough to almost see her face. She nodded, impressed. This was one of the cleaner ones. A passing grade, for sure. She turned and walked out.

Back at the office, she said, "I'll take it."

"Like it, do yuh?"

"Spotless."

"Thank you. One night?" the man asked.

"Yes, just the one."

"That'll be four dollars. Check out time is ten o'clock."

"I'll be long gone before that."

"So, one of those Phillips 66 girls, are yuh?"

"Yes, I am."

"We had one come through here a few weeks ago."

"That so."

"She seemed to like the place, too."

"Good. If I like it, I may be back." She sighed. "How's the cafe?"

"The best around," he quickly answered. "My wife runs the place. Good food."

"I'll try it."

"Yuh come far today?"

"Yes, I did."

"Where yuh headed?"

"West," she said.

"Would you like a wake-up call? We rent out alarm clocks."

Betty smiled. "No, thank you. I brought my own."

The man grinned and nodded. "Good thinking, young lady."

The next morning, Betty was up by seven, showered, and ate a breakfast of poached eggs on toast. Back at the front desk, the cheery gray-haired man sent her off. *Thanks for stopping in. You drive careful now. Come see us when you're through this way again.* The next stop was the Phillips 66 station on the other side of Springfield, which she reached forty-five minutes later.

She grabbed her clipboard from the front seat and stepped from her Plymouth. It was cooler than yesterday, not a cloud in the sky.

"Morning, doll," said a teenage gas jockey, jogging out to meet her. He saw the patch on her coat, and stopped cold.

"Look, kid, don't call me doll," Betty snapped. "I'm at least ten years older than you."

"Sorry," he apologized.

"I'm from head office. I'm sure you know what I'm here for." She removed her sunglasses, eyeing the station. She saw right off that the place was badly in need of some fresh paint. The pumps as well as the building. The white stucco and red trim—the company colors—was peeling. And the windows were dirty, to boot. It was time to be professional. "I'm here to inspect your restrooms," she said as cheerfully as she could.

"Yes. . . ma'am."

"Is anything wrong?"

"Why should anything be wrong?"

"Are they locked?"

"No, ma'am."

"Would you mind telling me where they are?"

"Around the back."

"Thank you."

"What's the matter, Jay?"

Betty turned at the sound of the voice. An overweight man in his forties, wearing a grubby Phillips 66 cap and dirty shirt emerged from the station.

"Well, lookee here. Can we help you, young lady?"

"You the manager?"

"Yes, ma'am."

"Then you must know why I'm here?"

The manager glanced over at the teenager, then back to the tall, attractive woman in white, a few inches taller than he was. "Well, you see, I was just about to get around to cleaning it."

Betty's lips formed into a half-smile, half-frown. She stared hard at him. "You have a co-ed restroom, I take it?"

"Yes, ma'am."

"May I see it, please."

"If you insist. Stay here, boy, and look after things."

"Sure, boss."

The manager took her to the back of the station. As they turned the corner, Betty saw the dingy *restroom* sign—crooked and hanging by one nail—over the cracked door frame. The door was peeling something awful. He turned the handle for her. She flicked on the light, and stood at the door. . . in awe. Grease coated the walls. The sink had a thick ring of dirt around it. There was loose plaster in the corner from a water leak above that left a three-foot-long stain on the ceiling. By far, this was the worst restroom she had seen in her two weeks on the job.

"What did you do, change a motor in here?" she wanted to know. "This is disgusting."

"I told you I was going to clean it up," the manager said, as strongly as he could. "Besides, the last one of you girls who came through cleaned it up herself."

She spun around. She had met this type before. Taking a breath, she said, firmly, "Clean it? Try blowing it up, first. I'm afraid to even touch the seat for fear of contracting some sort of disease." She began to scribble some notes on the paper attached to her clipboard. "According to our records, you've been fined before. Is that true?"

The manager took several seconds to answer. "Yes, ma'am, it is."

"One hundred dollars. This time head office won't be so lenient. You could be facing a fine of *five* hundred dollars."

He gripped her writing arm lightly. "Look it. Maybe we can come to an understanding."

She scratched her chin. "A deal, you mean?" She waited for the answer.

"Call it whatever you want. Give me a passing mark. I'll give you two hundred on the spot and you can pocket it." He was grinning now.

"Let me get this straight. You're bribing me?"

"Oh, no. I'm. . . making things easier for you."

"Oh, aren't you the perfect gentleman."

"Take the two hundred, move on and no one will know a thing. What yuh say, sweetie?"

She looked down at his hand still on her. "Don't call me *sweetie*. And, while you're at it, take your hairy, grimy little hands off me."

"Come on, babe." He slid his hand up her arm towards her shoulder and down the front of her neck. "Three hundred, then. How about it?"

Betty watched his roving hand and let the manager go as far as the top of her breast. *That was it.* To his complete shock, she stepped back and kneed him in the crotch with such force that the crunch echoed off the building. Then she backed away a few feet. The manager buckled over in pain, falling to his knees. He closed his eyes, and grunted and moaned several times, holding onto himself. She stood away at a safe distance, hands on her hips, until he finally opened his eyes and looked up at her.

She shook her head as he fell on his side.

Walking away, she said over her shoulder, without remorse, "See you, sport. You better be checking the papers for another job."

"Bitch!" he said, in parting, catching his breath.

She stopped and turned on her heels. "What did you say?"

"You heard me! Bitch!"

She wanted to respond, but decided to just keep going until she came upon the gas jockey standing at one of the pumps, watching a car approaching the station. "I think your boss could use an ice pack," she said, breezing past him. "Make it a large one."

She climbed into her Plymouth and roared away in a cloud of dust. On the road, she glanced back at the station in the rear-view mirror.

She took a deep breath and wiped her brow. Then. . . tears quickly came to her eyes. She wiped them slowly with the back of her shaking hand. Another mile on the road, the jolt of it had finally settled in and she cried out loud to herself. Head office will hear about this.

Damn, will they ever hear about this.

TULSA, OKLAHOMA

Betty crossed over the Kansas-Oklahoma border late morning, the next day. The sky was overcast. She drove straight on through and stopped for lunch at a Route 66 diner near a car dealership, and took a booth for two by the window. She hated eating at counters. Too close to the noise of the kitchen. She was hungry and ordered the soup of the day—mushroom—and a bacon-and-lettuce sandwich. Seventy cents on the menu. Out the window, she saw people on the sidewalks. Cars were driving past on the four lanes. This was a busy section of Tulsa. Across the street and down a few buildings sat a movie theater where—according to the neon—*Citizen Cane* was playing, a movie she had seen.

When the waitress left, Betty wiped her face with her hand. She was still shaking from the incident at the gas station. She had already made a long distance phone call to her employer who promised something would be done about the owner. She hoped. She waited, staring out the window. . . *thinking*. . . about *this new job*. . . Would another incident like the one two days ago occur again? Would she handle it the same way? Or was this just an isolated case?

Then. . . a tap on her shoulder made her jump.

"Hi yuh, Hostess McDougald."

She turned to look. It was Tony with a black sports coat draped over his arm. He was all dressed up. Clean, freshly-pressed white shirt. Dark green slacks, light green tie. Hair neatly combed. But still greasy. "Tony."

"Did I scare you?"

"Yes, you did."

"Sorry."

"What are you doing, following me?"

"Hell no." He laughed. "Mind if I join yuh?"

"Not at all."

"Thanks."

"I thought you'd be in Oklahoma City by now."

"I took a little detour. Thought I'd try my luck at job hunting here in Tulsa." He sat down. He seemed to be excited about something. "Mind if I smoke?"

"Go ahead. It's your health."

He lit a cigarette. Her order came. He asked for a hamburger with cheese and fries. Lots of gravy on the fries, he said to the waitress.

"So, how have things been since I saw you last?"

"No problems at all," she lied, drinking from a glass of water. "Everything's all peachy. What about you?"

He gently touched his hand to hers. "You know, I took your advice."

"How's that?" The manager at the gas station still fresh in her mind, she took her hand away slowly after a moment or two so casually that Tony didn't notice. She began to sip her soup.

"Try something new. Remember? Anyway, I think I got a job here in Tulsa."

"Really. Doing what?"

"Selling cars at the Chevrolet dealership, yonder."

She eyed the car lot through the wide glass windows. "Well, what do you know. Ever sell cars before?"

"Nope. But I can learn."

"Sure. Why not? You can start by enrolling in a crash course on engine troubleshooting."

"Ooh, that hurt," he grinned.

"Sorry. So, when will you know if you got the job?"

"Another hour. They told me to come back at one o'clock."

"I wish you all the best."

"Thanks."

Tony looked over her shoulder to the waitress coming towards them, a plastic tray in her hands. She stopped by their booth. "There you are, sir."

"Hey," Tony said. "That was fast. Looks good."

They ate and talked, until Tony had to leave.

Betty found it hard to believe that an hour had passed already. She watched Tony through the window as he jay-walked across the street to the boulevard between the four lanes. Drinking a second cup of coffee, she continued to watch him as he waited patiently for an opening in

44

the traffic. Nice guy, she thought. Real nice guy. Someone she wouldn't mind getting to know better.

Then. . . she saw it all.

A car came speeding up the street towards Tony, the driver going far too fast. Tony was just about to throw his suit jacket on, looking the other way, still on the boulevard, when the car jumped the curb and struck Tony, hurtling him into one of the near lanes. The oncoming car in the lane pounded on the brakes, barely missing Tony. Then the speeding car continued on, the driver attempting to make the turn at the intersection a hundred feet away. To the horror of those watching, he never made it. He crashed—dead on—into a telephone pole on the corner.

In seconds, traffic came to an abrupt halt on both sides of the road.

Betty jumped to her feet and ran to the counter. "Call an ambulance! Right away!" she told the two waitresses there. The next thing. . . *the first-aid kit in her car.* She ran for it and made her way through the crowd now assembling on the street.

"Let me through," she said, nudging past several people, concentrating on Tony first. "I'm a nurse."

She bent over him, the kit by her side. Tony was unconscious and on his side in a clump. She checked for a pulse. It was strong. Thank God for that. Tony's arm was bleeding through his shirt. She ripped at the material, careful not to move him, until she came to the slice in his arm. It was bad. As calmly as she could, she reached into the kit for the dressing package, even though she knew she had to hurry. The blood was actually pumping out before her eyes. She opened the dressing and made sure she didn't touch any surface that would come in contact with the wound. Then she bandaged the gauze pad firmly into position to control the bleeding and fastened the ends with the pin provided.

"Stand back. Give him some air. Leave him where he is," she exclaimed. "And for heaven's sake, don't touch him!" She grabbed her first aid kit and stood. "An ambulance will be coming shortly." Then she ran across the street, dodging the throng of people milling around.

When she arrived at the crashed vehicle, she stopped several feet back. A man and a woman were in front, slumped to the passenger side. The windshield was smashed in. Betty caught a whiff of hard liquor and saw a bottle in the back seat. The ages of the couple were hard to distinguish due to the blood covering them both from head to waist. The man had hit the telephone pole with the left side of the car, where the steering mechanisms were, and this was the reason the steering wheel ended up near the roof at approximately the spot where the driver's head should have been. Looking closer at the man, Betty could see that his head was nearly ripped away from the force of the wheel. It was a grizzly sight, something Betty had never seen in her nursing years. She could feel something strange in her stomach.

She swallowed hard, turned away quickly and threw up on the sidewalk. Then she pulled herself together and managed to check the pulse of the woman through the open passenger window. As she expected, she was dead, too. Betty backed away, wiping her mouth.

"Miss?" A man had to say it twice before Betty had comprehended it. "Miss?"

"What?" she said, staring at him.

"The fellow on the street is coming out of it."

"I'll be right over."

Betty ran to the boulevard. Tony was trying to get up, screaming in obvious pain.

Betty dropped to her knees over him. "Tony. It's me, Betty. Listen, don't move. An ambulance is coming. Lay down. OK."

He opened his eyes and tried to smile, but it was too difficult. "Give me something, Betty. Please, I can't take it. It hurts! It hurts!"

"Your arm?"

"Yeah. . . yeah, my arm."

"How's your chest and your head?"

"It's my arm! My arm!"

Betty was only following proper medical procedure. Never give morphine to anyone with a head or a chest injury. And never to anyone unconscious. She flipped the lid of the kit, snatched the small morphine stellate, removed the cap, and quickly found a clean area of fleshy skin above his waist by pulling out his shirt. She pinched the skin between her thumb and forefinger, and pushed the needle into the skin. Next, she squeezed the tube empty and slowly withdrew the needle.

"Give it a minute or two before it kicks in," she said. "Stay with me, Tony."

46

Tony didn't reply. Inside of two minutes the ambulance arrived with the police right behind them.

"You saw it all, did you?" the policeman asked Betty on the sidewalk in front of the restaurant. Tony had been taken away to the hospital. But there was still a large crowd circled around the smashed car down the street.

"Yes I did," she replied. "The driver struck Tony, spinning him into oncoming traffic. But the cars managed to stop in time. Then the driver—in the car that hit him—sped up and tried to turn at the corner."

The policeman shook his head and frowned, writing on a note pad. "But he didn't make it."

"That's right, officer."

"You know the man who was hit, is that correct?"

"Not really. We're not friends, or anything like that. I met him on the road in Missouri, then by chance here in Tulsa."

"I see."

Another policeman walked up and stood beside the one asking Betty questions. "I got the dead couple's ID," he said, glancing at a driver's license inside a blood-stained wallet. "The man is Walter Buchanan. Twenty-eight years old. From St. Louis. Address is—"

"*Who* did you say?" Betty interrupted.

"Walter Buchanan."

Betty rubbed her forehead. This was not her day.

"Are you all right, miss? You don't look so good."

Later that evening in the hospital, Betty found Tony's room. It was visiting hours now. Tony saw her at the doorway, still in her hostess uniform.

"Betty." He smiled, leaning on his good side.

She strolled gracefully into the room, past one other bed where a patient was sleeping. "Hi, kiddo."

"That's the second time you came to my rescue. Thanks."

"You're welcome."

"The doctor said I might have bled to death if you didn't apply the bandage."

Betty stood by the bed rail, looking down at Tony in his hospital gown, the sheets below his waist. He was very pale. "Just doing my job."

He chuckled. "You take everything so casual."

It was her turn to chuckle, remembering how she had vomited on the sidewalk earlier.

"How yuh feeling? Anything broken?"

He moved slowly, rustling the sheets. "No. Just a lot of bruises and scrapes. They say it was a miracle."

"I'll say."

"I still can't figure how I was so badly cut."

"Could have been something sharp on the car that did it."

"Yeah, I suppose."

There was an awkward silence, until he asked, "I guess you'll be back on the road."

"Yes." She looked away. He reached for her arm and held on.

"Will we ever see each other again?"

Betty took a long time to answer. "I don't know. . . why would you ask?"

"Because I think I'm falling in love with you." Then he tried to yank her down to him.

She resisted, pulling away.

"Betty, please."

"I don't even know your last name, for heaven's sake."

"So?"

"Tony," she uttered, clearing her throat, "I must go."

"Wait! Just like that?"

She turned and walked away, without looking back at the crushed young man. She didn't stop until she hurried to the parking lot and unlocked her Phillips 66 Plymouth company car. She leaned back in her seat and sighed. She had to leave the hospital. She had to end the relationship then and there.

That was the best.

She started the car and let it idle. She smiled slow and wide, although the situation wasn't that funny. Only weird. Was somebody up there trying to tell her something? But what? It was too much of a coincidence. How could she have told Tony that Walter Buchanan—the drunken maniac behind the wheel—was her ex-husband?

It would have been far, far too cruel.

48

4

Strange Bedfellows

The Second World War brought a swift change to traffic on Route 66. With gas rationing on, there were fewer cars and more trucks. Military trucks. Contractor trucks. Those working for the military. The Mother Road became a major thruway for the American war machine as well as a getaway for one certain individual who had plans to sell what he had stolen.

WICHITA, KANSAS—JANUARY, 1945

A man in an expensive double-breasted suit hurried across the floor of the giant factory. He meandered in and out of the line of silver bombers and busy technicians, heading to the far corner, where the stairs led to the second-level meeting rooms. In every direction, the activity continued on first thing in the morning. Hammering, drilling, shouts from supervisors. It was here that Boeing was building the largest and most advanced aircraft of the war, the B-29 Superfortress, a bomber the world had not seen up to that time. It had onboard computers that operated the guns. It had pressurized compartments. It could hit a target—drop a bomb into a pickle barrel—at thirty-thousand feet. The press had tagged it the Billion Dollar Bomber.

The man frowned, ascended the stairs two at a time, hoping earnestly that the two billion dollars spent to date hadn't been flushed down the toilet. He took to the long hall, and opened the fourth door on the right. Inside were two men seated across from each other at a long, polished table.

"Well, Shaw, what's the news?" one of them asked, impatiently.

"You won't like it."

"Where is he? He was supposed to be here fifteen minutes ago with the new engine plans."

"I can't find him," Shaw answered.

The two men at the table exchanged hardened glances. A young, shapely, dark-haired woman in a tight blue dress opened the door and looked at Shaw.

"Yes, Miss Doyle," Shaw said, "what is it? I hope you have some good news."

"No, sir, I don't. He's nowhere to be found."

"Blasted! Did you call the house he's renting?"

"Yes, sir. His landlady said he drove away over an hour ago."

Shaw grunted. "Thank you, Miss Doyle. You may go."

"Yes, sir."

She shut the door.

Shaw turned to the other two. "I hope this isn't what I think it is."

"It may be," one of them said.

"If that's the case, we better call security. Now!"

One of the men scrambled for the phone in the corner.

OKLAHOMA

Peter Benning—real name Wolfgang Muller—lit a cigarette with his butane lighter and glanced in the rear-view mirror of his Packard sedan. No one was following him. Not a car for miles on this stretch of two-lane gravel. He puffed his smoke, both hands on the wheel. He sped up, despite the snowy patches on the road of this bleak, prairie countryside in the middle of an Oklahoma winter.

They're coming, he thought to himself. No doubt. They're coming.

He clicked the radio on and caught a morning war news report. Same old thing on the Eastern Front. A major offensive north of Warsaw meant the Soviets were pushing closer to Germany's borders. To the west, Patton and the British Allies in the XXX Corps joined up near St Hubert, France. In the Philippines, the US 25th Division had landed at Lingayen. Serious fighting. Kamikaze attacks on American shipping.

He flicked the radio off. He saw an airplane ahead—a mile away—banking away from him. The wing structure told him it was an AT-6, probably from a nearby Army Air training base.

WICHITA

Two men in trench coats and fedoras approached Miss Doyle at her desk. One was much taller and darker, in his thirties. But it was the other one—the older man of the two—who seemed to be in charge.

"Yes," Miss Doyle said, looking up from her shiny, black Underwood typewriter.

The older, shorter man removed his fedora. The other man followed with the same courtesy. "I'm Fallon. This is Barkley," the short man said. "We came to see Mr. Shaw."

"Security?"

"Yes."

"You may go right in. Mr. Shaw is expecting you."

"Thank you."

The men entered the room, the secretary closing the door behind them. Shaw rose to his feet. Fallon flashed his pocket identification the way a police detective would.

In an instant, the blood drained from Shaw's face. "OSS?"

"Yes, sir."

"What gives? Where's our plant security?"

Fallon returned the ID to the breast pocket of his suit. "It's over their heads. We've taken over. What we have here may be an international incident."

"Tell me straight out. Is Benning a spy?"

"That's very possible, yes."

"I always thought he looked German. That blonde, blue-eyed Nazi bastard!"

Fallon took in the remark with a sardonic smirk. "We have to keep a lid on everything we do. No bulletins. No pictures in the papers. Nothing. Is that understood?"

"Yes. Whatever you say."

"Is anything missing?"

"Blueprints."

"What blueprints in particular?"

Shaw sighed. "The new B-29 cylinder heads."

"Is there anything significant about these new cylinder heads?"

"You're damn right there is. They keep the engine temperatures down to a very tolerable level. The B-29 has had heating problems in combat for months. These cylinder heads could revolutionize the military aircraft industry. Light weight magnesium that can take the heat."

"I see," Fallon remarked. "So, if they fall into enemy hands, then they—"

"Do you know what it's like for the B-29 pilots out there in the Pacific?" Shaw went on. "Do you? The allowable head temperatures were originally supposed to be 265 degrees. Maximum. Reports tell me that no one keeps the temperatures below 300 on take-off. So. . . engines are overheating and catching fire. The planes are blowing up before they can even get off the ground."

"That's terrible."

"Tell me something, if you could?" Shaw asked.

"What's that?"

"Providing Benning is a spy, what good are these blueprints by themselves? Germany will obviously lose the war. Japan is next. The blueprints will do neither side any good this late."

Fallon eyebrows flickered. "Strange, isn't it."

"Well?"

"I'm not at liberty to answer that. In the meantime, shut your people up. We'll find Benning for you."

"I sure as hell hope so. Or we both better be looking for other jobs."

South of Wichita

Barkley had two maps spread out in his lap on the passenger side. He looked to Fallon behind the wheel of the car. "You think Muller's making an escape?"

Fallon kept his eyes on the snowy, prairie road. "Yeah. Seems so."

"Geez." Barkley shook his head. "After all the things we've done for him. Got him on our side. Trained him, given him a new start, a new name."

"But he's still a German. I've always suspected him."

"And I think he knew it."

"Yeah."

"Which way do you think he's traveling?" Barkley looked down at one of the maps.

"If you were him, what would you do?"

Barkley shrugged. "Eastern seaboard is too far. So's the west. South, I'd guess. Mexico."

"Exactly what I was thinking. Now. . . which way exactly? Seeing that he doesn't know the ropes around here that well, he's probably taking the most obvious. Route 66 as far as he can, then straight south to the border. Probably through El Paso and Juarez."

"Juarez? Hey. . . isn't that where that German agent. . . what's his name. . . Kiel. . . operates?"

"You got it."

"I remember Muller's file. They know each other, don't they?"

Fallon nodded. "They were a team. Switzerland. South America. Mexico. Both learned their trade from the masters. The good ol' Gestapo."

"What the hell is Muller up to?"

"That's for us to find out." Fallon slowed down for a T in the road. "How far to the Oklahoma border?"

Barkley consulted the map. "Five miles. Maybe less."

Outside Oklahoma City

Wolfgang Muller jammed coins into the slots at the gas station phone booth.

"I will connect the call now, sir," the operator said.

"Thank you, operator," Muller replied, with no German accent.

Juarez, Mexico—across the Rio Grande from El Paso, Texas

The telephone rang in the darkened bedroom. A man's arm slid out from under the covers and reached for the receiver on the nightstand by the bed.

"Hello," the man said.

"Henry?" The voice said. "It's me, Wolf."

The man sat up, quickly. "Wolf? How do I know it's you?"

"Land lover."

The man turned to the naked woman in bed with him. "Get lost," he said, kicking her out and onto the tiled floor.

Fuming, the woman swore at him in Spanish. Then she reached for her robe on the floor to cover herself.

"Where are you?" the man asked.

"Oklahoma City. I have something. Big. Real big. Can we meet half-way?"

"Wait five minutes. Call me back."

He heard the click in his ear.

OUTSIDE OKLAHOMA CITY

Muller nodded, and wrote down the information on a note pad. "See you there," he said into the receiver. He hung up and smiled.

He looked across the busy highway to the road sign that read OKLA-HOMA US 66.

OKLAHOMA CITY

Fallon eased off the gas pedal. They were on a busy street.

"The sign for Route 66 should be coming up soon," Barkley notified his associate. "This Kiel fellah, who is he, anyway?"

"Don't you know?"

Barkley shook his head. "Not really."

"He's the best German agent operating out of Mexico. He's been there since Pearl Harbor. Any German agent in the States with information seeks him out. He has connections. A lot of his info is passed on to Berlin through the German Embassy in Mexico City. His real name is Heinrich Staffen. Born in Kiel."

Barkley nodded. "Ah, that's why the name."

"Yep."

They stopped at a traffic light.

Fallon pointed ahead. "There it is. The sign. Route 66. A block up."

"You sure he's taking this way?"

"Positive," Fallon assured his associate. "Remember. . . we're looking for a black Chevy sedan. Kansas license. . . BL 1145."

"Got yuh. But what if he switches plates? Maybe even cars? Then what?"

"I don't think he will."

"Why not?"

"I just don't think he will."

"But he does have two hours on us."

"True. We'll make it up, though."

"I still can't figure something out."

"What's that?" Fallon asked.

"Like Shaw said, what good are the B-29 blueprints to the Germans or even the Japs? They can't really do anything with them."

The light changed and they were mobile again, closing in on the Route 66 sign.

"Yeah," Fallon agreed. "That doesn't make sense. Unless. . ."

"Unless what?"

"He's selling to someone else."

"Who?"

"Wait a second."

Fallon yanked the car over to the curb, and jammed on the brakes.

"What yuh do that for?"

Fallon pointed through the windshield at the sign only a few feet away. "Look."

They both saw that the bottom of the metal sign had a strip of masking tape and an arrow—a ball-point pen marking—pointing right. Below the arrow was the initials WM.

"He's up to his old tricks."

"Yeah," Fallon agreed. "He's giving us clues to where he goes. Why does everything have to be a game with him? That's how we caught him in the first place."

"So he doesn't know we're following him, eh?"

Fallon glanced over his left shoulder and gunned the car, turning the corner and screeching the tires. They were now on Route 66, but still in traffic.

"You were saying he could be selling to someone else," Barkley reminded Fallon.

"Yeah. . . the Russians."

"Are you serious? I thought they're our allies."

Fallon grunted and stopped for another light. "Some allies. Did you know that a couple B-29 crews had been forced to land in Russian territory after bombing Japan? No one has heard from them. One of the B-29s was sent into the water and the crew bailed out. The other was nearly intact after a proper landing. Washington figures the Russians will keep it and build a carbon copy of it. If that's the case, then Moscow could use these new blueprints to help them along."

"Maybe so. But are they gonna buy them from a German, who they're at war with?"

"From a smart German who knows his Fatherland is *kaput*? Hell, yeah. Why not?"

"I see what you mean. Strange business we're in."

Near Amarillo, Texas

Muller stood by his car on the gravel shoulder and glanced around. He was outside the city. He quickly placed a piece of masking tape at the bottom of the Route 66 sign. With a ball-point pen, he drew an arrow pointing left, and another pointing down.

Then he got into his car and drove away.

Barkley and Fallon arrived at the same spot less than two hours later and stared at the sign, while they both emerged from the car.

"Two arrows this time," Barkley said.

"What's he trying to do?"

"Throw us, I bet."

"No." Fallon bent down and moved his hand through the gravel until he came upon a white envelope. "Well, lookee here." He opened the flap to find a letter inside. "This is why the one arrow was down."

Barkley looked over his shoulder to read for himself. "Geez, he's telling us exactly where to meet him."

"Yeah, the bus depot in Albuquerque. Tomorrow morning. Eight thirty."

"Think it's a trap?"

Fallon took several seconds to answer. "I don't know. He's really acting goofy this time."

Tucumcari, New Mexico

Muller checked in at the motel office after nightfall, where a rough, overweight, middle-aged woman sat behind the front desk.

She smiled, cigarette dangling from her mouth. "Good evening."

"Good evening," Muller answered. "I'd like a room, please, for the night."

She turned behind her to a set of keys clipped on the wall. "Sure. Number fourteen. Down to the right. That will be six bucks."

He opened his wallet, paid the woman, and took the key. "Thank you, ma'am."

"We have a ten-thirty AM checkout here."

"You bet."

Muller strode out the office door and found the room down the concrete walkway. He unlocked the door, but when he turned the handle, he found the door was stuck. With a slight shove, and a squeak, he entered, flicked the light on and threw the suitcase on the bed. He closed the curtains, locked the door using the latch, and opened his suitcase. He stared down at the clothes. . . the large manila envelope containing the B-29 blueprints. . . and a .38-caliber pistol complete with silencer.

ALBUQUERQUE, MEXICO

Kiel sat down hard in a restaurant booth beside the window. A glance at his watch told him it was eight-ten. No clouds. Quite chilly this sunny morning. About forty degrees. He saw the bus depot across the street, hoping his friend would make it. He heard light footsteps and looked up at a cute, blonde waitress in a long skirt and baggy blouse. In her hands was a pen and a pad of paper, ready for her early morning customer.

"Hi there, mister, what'll it be?"

"Bacon, two eggs, toast. Coffee. Make it black." He glanced again to the outside.

She wrote on the pad. "OK. Coming right up. Hey," she said, hands on hips, "you expecting someone?"

"Why do you ask that?"

"You keep looking out the window."

"Maybe I *am* expecting someone. Is that a problem for you?" Kiel attempted a weak grin.

"No, just curious."

"Now, may I have my breakfast, please."

She shrugged. "Sure."

In the parking lot behind the bus depot, Barkley and Fallon spotted Muller's black Chevy.

"There she be," Barkley said, walking over to the rear bumper. "BL 1145. So, he didn't ditch it after all."

Fallon's keen eyes shot around the lot, taking everything in. Cars and buses filled half the area. "I still don't like this. Something stinks." He saw a clear view of the moderate traffic on the street. "Geez!"

"What?"

Fallon reached over and pushed Barkley down with him behind the passenger door. Then he slowly looked over the door, through the windshield, to the street. "There he is. Muller."

"Yuh sure it's him?"

"Positive."

"Did he see us?"

"No. I don't think so."

Barkley remained where he was.

"What's he doing?"

"He's walking across the street. . . into the restaurant."

"What should we do?"

"Follow him. Come on, get up!"

"Wait. Shit!"

"What's the matter now?"

"Company. Someone came out. Stay down! They're talking. I can't get a good look at the other one. Wait, he's turning around. They're walking into the alley. Oh, shit! It's him!"

"Who?"

"Kiel."

"What!"

"I'd recognize him anywhere. Geez, Kiel is here in Albuquerque. We got the two of them! Together! I don't believe it."

"Kiel. . . here?"

"I think the pieces are coming together, now. I get it. Muller gave us clues to follow him. He's working for us after all."

"You think so."

"He's leading us right to Kiel."

In the alley between the restaurant and the next building—a pawn shop—Muller pumped the hand of his old friend and hugged him.

"Heinrich. Heil Hitler."

Kiel smiled back. "Heil Hitler. It's good to see you, Wolfgang. You made it."

"Yes. I saw you in the window."

"Let's go to my auto. It's behind the restaurant."

They walked as casually as they could to Kiel's Ford convertible, and they climbed into the vehicle. Kiel lit a cigarette and rolled his window down. "Where have you been for the last year? Nobody has heard from you?"

"I've been hiding out."

"So, what do you have for me?"

"Blueprints to the new B-29 Superfortress engines." Muller dug the manila envelope from under his shirt.

Kiel opened the envelope and saw what was inside. Large blueprints, folded up. "What good are these blueprints to Germany? The B-29 means nothing to us."

"They will."

"In what way?"

"The other side could use them. Heinrich, stop kidding yourself. Germany has lost the war. The Russians could use this new design. And they will pay handsomely for it."

"The Russians!"

"Yes, of course."

Muller happened to glance in the side mirror. He thought he saw someone move in and out of the cars in the lot, staying down low. *It was them.* They had caught up to him, as expected. Slowly, he felt inside his suit jacket for the pistol strapped to his chest.

"What's the matter?" Kiel said.

"I hear someone."

A man jumped up out of nowhere and pulled on the passenger door handle. Another man popped up on the driver's side. Both men were armed, guns pointed into the car. Muller recognized the man closest to him. "Herr Fallon. What kept you?"

"Both of you, out of the car," Fallon ordered. "Now!"

The two Germans obeyed. They could see that the two Americans now had their guns hidden under their coats, barrels out.

"Don't try anything, Kiel." Fallon turned to Muller. "Good work, Muller. You lead him right to us. It was a clever plan you put together."

"You figured it out, did you?" Muller said, stepping over to where Barkley and Fallon were standing, leaving Kiel alone.

"You pig, Wolfgang!"

"Yes. It all came to me this morning," Fallon said, "once I saw your old friend. But why did you take the B-29 blueprints with you? You did take them, didn't you?"

Muller smiled. "Yes, I did. I had to flush you out and I knew that security would send for you—my case officer—to find me."

"Your case officer," Kiel said. "How long has this been?"

"A year, Heinrich," Muller replied. "They convinced me of the error of my ways."

"That's why no one's heard from you."

"Yes, Heinrich."

"Traitor!"

"Let's go, Kiel. You're not in Mexico now," Fallon said. "Turn around. Hands behind your back. Barkley, get out the cuffs."

"Right."

Barkley removed a set of cuffs from his coat. It was the perfect screen for Muller, who calmly reached for his pistol, withdrew it, and fired at the Americans point blank. Two thumps—barely audible—and they both hit the ground, blood spots on their chests.

Speechless, Kiel turned to his friend.

"I've waited a year to do that," Muller said, standing over them. He then fired two more into each body for good measure.

"Then it was only an act, my friend?"

Muller slid the gun into his chest harness. "Yes, Heinrich, it was."

Kiel grabbed Muller by the arm. "Get in the auto. Quick, come with me."

"Where we going? Mexico?"

Kiel smiled. "Where else? We'll talk about the Russians."

"Yes, let's."

Kiel stopped, his hand on the driver's door handle. "It's good to have you back."

Muller blinked at his friend. "It's good to be back. We have lots to talk about."

"Indeed. Get in."

As Kiel drove off, Muller said, "the war is over. It's every man for himself now."

5

The All-Stars

The war was over in Europe. Japan was next, a month away from the atomic bombs on Hiroshima and Nagasaki. Even during the war years baseball remained America's Pastime. However, it was a different game in the summer of 1945 when blacks did not play alongside whites in pro ball.

NEAR VEGA, TEXAS—JULY, 1945

Seth Lucas clambered aboard the team bus outside the ball park. Along with the other colored ballplayers still in uniform, he was bone tired after the double-header in the ninety-degree heat. By now, half-way into the barnstorming season, he had gotten used to—or just plain put up—with many things. The smell of sweaty bodies on the bus after the games. Meals of hot dogs and warm pop. Day after day in uniform before he could shower. Even then, cleaning up was usually acted out in a colored section somewhere, complete with mediocre-to-bad plumbing.

Seth plunked himself down in an empty seat on the middle-right and slid to the open window. At last, at eight o'clock, it was starting to cool down. Tomorrow would be a day off. Thank God. But a long ride was ahead for the next game in Joplin, Missouri, the day after that. A day's rest would be a gift for the sore knee he'd been nursing.

The crowd today—mostly white folk in cowboy hats and boots—had enjoyed the afternoon spectacle. Seth's team, the Texas All-Stars, put on an entertaining show, taking on a local white team in oil country.

Shadow Ball was the fan favorite, where the infield played with an imaginary ball during the warm up. On the sidelines, one of the players played catch by throwing two balls at the same time to two of his teammates. In the fourth inning, the center fielder caught a long out in his cap, of all places. The pitcher waved in the outfielders in the third inning. Then. . . the first batter struck out. The next two grounded out. All on eight pitches. The catcher caught the fifth inning in a rocking chair. The fans loved the entire performance, not minding at all that the colored team had beaten their local nine by a six-run margin. It was entertainment. And they paid for it. That was all that counted.

Seth Lucas was one of two rookies, the youngest member on the team at eighteen, a short, wiry, fast-as-a-deer shortstop. He hated the clowning side of colored ball. He wanted to play the serious stuff. But people weren't paying money here in Vega—or elsewhere along the circuit—for that. Colored were supposed to be clowns. So, he had settled in, like the others on the bus. It was a living, pitiful as it was.

"How's the knee, kid?" Jay Westlake asked, sitting down beside Seth. Westlake was one of the veterans on the club, the first baseman. Nearing thirty-five, he was over six feet tall, broad-shouldered, wide above the waist, and the slugger on the team. He was also the player-manager. "I see you were still limping out there."

"It's getting better."

"Good crowd out there, today."

"Not bad."

The bus began to move onto the road and speed up.

Westlake folded his arms across his chest. "It gets to yuh after a while, don't it?"

"What?"

"The traveling."

"Yeah. Suppose so." Seth's eyes stayed glued to the road.

Westlake nudged his young teammate. "Not much for talking, are yuh?"

"Nope."

Westlake flipped his cap over his eyes. "Me neither. I'm bushed."

Unable to close his eyes, Seth watched the scenery in silence while Westlake slept. Four teammates played cards in the seats behind him. Seth listened to the ball stories they were telling. Names were mentioned. *Satchel Paige. Josh Gibson. Cool Papa Bell. Roy Campanella.* Some of the giants in the game. Players from the Negro major leagues, the league back east that Seth hoped to join one day. Gibson could smash long, arching home runs off any pitcher, black or white. Paige could strike out any batter, and often did it with the outfield called in. Bell could run like a deer. Then Seth sat up and listened intently when one of the players bragged that he and his pappy saw Bell once run from first to home on a bunt!

First to home on a bunt. Shit!

"It's true," the player said in earnest.

"Bull," answered one of the other players.

"No listen. Bell was on first. The batter bunted. The pitcher fielded the ball and threw to first. Bell flew around second and went for third because he saw that the third baseman had not gotten back to the bag yet. The catcher saw that the third baseman had not gotten back, so he went to cover at third. Bell saw that home was unoccupied, so he ran home."

"I still don't believe."

"I saw it! Honest!"

By nightfall the conversation died down. The bus turned onto Route 66 and headed west.

BETWEEN OKLAHOMA CITY AND TULSA

Seth saw the glow on the horizon before most of the others. It was two or three miles away in the night. As the driver drew closer and slowed down, he and most of his teammates now waking saw the three burning crosses in the field beside the highway.

"It's the Klan!" Wakefield said, terror in his voice. "They got the road blocked."

Seth bit his lip. "What do they want?"

"I dunno. As long as it's not us."

The bus had stopped dead now. Everyone was awake. Three cars were in front of them. About twenty Ku Klux Klan—in white hoods and garb—circled around the cars, talking with the occupants. One by one, each car was allowed through the blockade. The driver—old gray-haired Danny—moved the bus forward and stopped. Four Klansmen advanced forward, a purpose to their steps. One pounded on the door. When it opened, he and the three others climbed aboard. One man held a flashlight.

In the past, Seth had only seen Klan members from afar. Being this close scared the living daylights out of him. Besides, all he could see was white sheets and eyes. He recalled the stories he had heard back in his home state of Georgia. The cross burnings. The threats. The beatings. The lynchings. And now here they were in the same bus. The Klan members stared—taking a second or two—into each colored face. The one who pounded on the door walked slowly up and down the aisle, taking another look.

"Can we help yuh?" Danny asked, as calmly as he could.

"We're looking for a murderer, there pops," the Klan member in the aisle said, his voice muffled under the white hood. He shone his flashlight across the faces of the players in uniform. "A black man killed a white farmer down the road, not far from here. Then he ran. We want him."

"Ain't no murderers on this bus."

"Ball team, are yuh?"

"Yes, sir."

"Where yuh boys come from?"

"Vega, Texas."

"Where yuh headed?"

"Joplin, Missouri."

The man grunted. Then he turned and glanced at the other three, shaking his head. "OK, let these boys go," he said.

The Klan members left the bus. The group waved Danny through.

Seth and the others breathed a sigh a relief.

NEAR MIAMI, OKLAHOMA

Seth woke at sunup when Danny swung over to the gravel shoulder opposite a field of short grass. The bus had run out of gas in the middle of nowhere. Nearest farm had to be at least two miles away in the distance.

Danny shook his head, disgusted. Damn! The last two gas stations he had tried on Route 66 in the middle of the night wouldn't serve him. *Now what were they going to do?*

"Well, what now?" Westlake said to the team. No one had an answer. "Ah, shit, let's go take a breather."

The players, still in uniform, moaned and stretched as they all climbed out of the bus until it was empty. The eastern sun rising over the hills was a tonic against their faces after the night drive. One of the players pointed to a vehicle chugging towards them from the east.

"What yuh think, boss," Danny said to Westlake, "should we flag 'er down?"

"Nah. See if he stops first."

"OK."

They were in luck. It was a truck, two people inside. The driver screeched to a halt on the shoulder.

"You got trouble?" the driver shouted across the road, over the idling engine.

"Yeah, we do," Danny replied. "We done run out of gas."

"A ball team, are yuh?"

"Yes, sir."

The driver shut the motor off. The two people got out and slammed their doors. The truck had seen better days. At least ten years old, it was dented and unwashed. The driver—cigarette in mouth—appeared to be in his thirties. Long, greasy dark hair. Plaid shirt. The other was a muscular, blonde-haired youngster with blue eyes, in his early teens in a white T-shirt. Farmers, by their appearance. Both in denim pants.

"Yuh up early, ain't yuh?" Westlake asked, taking over as the team's spokesman.

The driver crossed the road with the teenager, and answered. "Going fishing with my boy, here."

"We got a problem."

"What's up?"

"No one wants to serve us any gasoline in these parts."

The father coughed and rubbed his chin. "Yeah, that's a problem all right, considering some of the folks round here. The gas rationing, too, yuh know."

"We're open to suggestions."

The father chuckled. "I bet you are. Hmm. Need gas, huh?"

"Yep."

He glanced back to his truck. "I got me a 50-gallon spare tank in the back of my truck, there, that I haul around."

"I noticed."

"Yuh know, I know someone who can fill 'er up. I can bring it back here, then you boys can syphon 'er. What you say to that?"

"We'd like that fine."

"Where yuh headed, fellahs?"

"Joplin, Missouri."

"That should get yuh there. Where'd yuh come from?"

"Texas. Other side of Amarillo."

"Long ways."

"Yeah."

"Now. . . trouble is, I need the money first." The father coughed again. "I figure fifty gallons should run yuh ten dollars. You got ten dollars?"

"Yeah. But how do we know you're gonna come back? We had it happen to us once before."

The father huffed. "Well, I guess you're just gonna have to trust me." Westlake looked around at his team.

Then the boy piped up. "I can stay, pa, till yuh get back. You know, as collateral."

"What!"

"Sure, pa, I'll stay."

"Come here." The father took his son away from the players and whispered, "Look here, boy, you don't know these people. They're—"

"I know, pa, they're colored," the boy whispered back. "But didn't you once tell me that it was what was in a person's heart that counts, not the color of his skin?"

"Yeah, well. . ."

"Around here, we know some good Cherokee Indians and some bad ones. Must be the same way with colored, too."

The father fell into silence, seeing the logic in his son's statement. "Yeah, I guess so."

The boy shrugged. "Anyway, they're ballplayers, pa."

The father considered his son's suggestion, glancing at the bus and the players. "So, you think it's OK as long as they're ball players, do yuh?"

"Sure."

"OK." The father coughed again, harshly this time. He reached for the cigarettes in his shirt pocket and lit one. "I'll get their money and be right back."

The father took the money, turned the truck around, and headed back down the road.

"Ball players, huh?" The youngster said, feeling the players out.

"Yeah, we are," Seth answered, stepping out of the pack of players. "How about you?"

"I play a little."

"What position?"

"Infield. Short, mostly. My pa plays too, on weekends. He's one of those semi-pros."

"What does he do the rest of the time? Farm?"

"Nah, he's a miner. Mined most of his life. Tried farming a year ago, just outside Commerce. He planted oats, wheat, corn. Had milking cows, too. But we got flooded out at harvest time. It rained for days and days. The crick behind our house backed up and ran over our property. It wiped us out. So, we went back to the mines. Moved back to town in Commerce. He hates it, though. Mining, that is. The dust is in his lungs. That's why he coughs a lot. His smoking don't help none, neither. I've tried to tell him that, but he don't listen to me, or my momma. Anyway, he doesn't want me or my brothers to go down under, as he calls it."

"What they mine here?"

"Lead and zinc."

"So what are you gonna do if yuh don't mine?"

"I'm going to be a ball player," the kid said firmly.

"That so?" Westlake said, displaying white teeth. "Well. . . what's you're favorite team?"

"The St. Louis Cardinals. I like Stan Musial."

"Good ballplayer."

"Yeah, you bet."

"Who's *your* favorite?" the kid asked.

"Ever hear of Josh Gibson?"

"Yeah, I have. Are all those stories about him true?"

"It depends what you've heard." Westlake took a deep breath. "Nice country around here, you know."

"Yeah, it is," the youngster agreed. "So, yuh headed to Joplin, Missouri, are yuh?"

"That's right."

"My pa tells me that there's so many mine shafts in these parts, that you can walk underground from here, clean all the way to Joplin."

A few of the players laughed.

Seth then asked, "How long will it take before your pa gets back?"

67

"I dunno for sure."

"You wanna play catch?"

The boy shrugged. "Sure."

"Let's see what you got."

"Gotta glove for me? I left mine in the back of the truck."

"I think I can rustle one up for yuh."

Soon, Seth and the youngster were throwing a stained yellow ball back and forth on the gravel shoulder, as the occasional vehicle came down the highway. Almost all the occupants slowed down and gawked at the spectacle. *A black man playing catch with a white boy.* After five minutes, Seth and the kid lengthened the distance between them until they were forty feet apart. The boy's throws were not that accurate but they were hard, snapping into Seth's glove. The other players watched, until one of them said, "Let's see if the kid can hit."

"How about it?" Seth said to the blonde boy.

"OK. I like hitting."

The boy and the players began to gather in the open, rectangular field next to the bus. It was bordered by a wire fence that in a pinch could substitute for a diamond, although there were several slight-to-moderate dips to the land. The morning began to warm as the sun rose in the eastern sky. The ground was soft, but not mushy, after a rain two days before. Fence post to fence post—perpendicular to the road—the grass field was well over three hundred feet long. One of the team's pitchers—a tall, gangly right-hander with ink-black skin—marched off the distance from home and marked a line in the grass with his cleat. The team's main catcher grabbed his face mask and found a long stick for home plate. Two other players went to the far end of the field to shag flies. Seth jogged over and stood whereabouts the shortstop would be. The boy took several practice cuts with a bat. The pitcher warmed up a bit, first by throwing a dozen or more pitches, then motioned for the kid to step up.

The kid dug in where a left-handed hitter's box would be and cocked his bat. With one steady, compact swing, he knocked the first pitch—a slow to medium fastball—over the fence and into a clump of trees at the far end of the field. Seth stood, surprised, staring at the trees, then back to the white kid. *Geez*, he thought, *that had to be a good four hundred feet. Easy.* He glanced over at the pitcher and their eyes met.

"Lucky hit," the pitcher said to Seth.

"Yeah, you're right," Seth answered, not so sure that it actually was luck. "Give him one with some zip, this time."

The pitcher threw one harder, belt high. A medium fastball. The kid punched this one between the two outfielders. The ball bounced to the fence on two hops. Both times there was a distinct, solid crack off the bat, the kind of sound that most ballplayers knew. The sound that spelled *base hit*. After a dozen more pitches, Seth and the others were amazed at the kid's power and batting eye. He was hitting everything. Curves. Fastballs. High. Low. On the corners of the plate. And the kid didn't even seem to be sweating. When the pitcher threw two in a row well off that plate—pitches that the kid didn't swing at—he stopped and took a deep breath.

"Sorry, kid, I don't want to throw my arm out," he said, strolling away to the side.

"Still wanna go, kid?" Seth called out loud from his shortstop position.

The kid, hands on his hips, called back, "Sure."

"Let's see what you can do with a lefty," Westlake said, motioning for the team's only left-handed pitcher to try a few.

The pitcher agreed. He was shorter and more powerfully built than the other pitcher. Like his predecessor, he too threw a few warm-up pitches. All of them were breaking balls that had lots of movement, but little speed. Many players referred to these type of pitches as *junk*, which even the best of hitters often had trouble with. Finished with his pitches, the junk man waited for the kid. Everyone in competitive baseball knew that left-handed hitters had trouble hitting left-handed pitchers. It was a fact. The battle lines were drawn. Lefty verse lefty. Black verse white. Adult verse kid, really. Then. . . to the surprise of the whole team, the kid stepped into the side of the imaginary box for right-handed hitters.

"Oh, crap. If that don't beat all," Seth cried. "He's a switch hitter."

The kid looked down at the catcher and grinned. "Did I do something wrong?"

The catcher chuckled. "Be patient kid. Jess be patient."

The kid smashed three in a row to the fence with that *sound* off the bat again. The fourth one cleared the trees by twenty feet.

Westlake waved his arms, jumping into the area between the catcher and the pitcher. "All right, that's enough. Damn, kid, who taught you to hit like that?"

"My pa."

"You got yerself a smart pa. You like hitting, do yuh?"

"Sure do. Just like I said."

"How old are yuh, anyway?"

"Thirteen, now. Fourteen in October."

"Geez. I wonder if Josh Gibson was that good at thirteen?"

The sound of a chugging truck broke the conversation. The kid's father had returned. In minutes, the gas was transferred from the truck to the bus. The players were ready to leave. Westlake thanked the farmer and his son.

"By the way, kid," Westlake said, as the father and son turned in the direction of the truck. "I hope you make it to the majors. You're good. Damn good."

The kid beamed, glancing at his dad. "Thanks."

"I hope you guys make it, too." Then he wanted to correct himself. "I mean one of you. I mean—" The boy's face flushed embarrassment.

"Forget it. We know what you mean. But it won't happen," Westlake said, sadly. "Not in our time."

The father lit a cigarette, and puffed. "You never know."

"How'd yuh learn to switch hit, kid?"

"My dad would pitch right to me, and my grandpa would pitch left."

Westlake smiled. "Keep it up."

"I will. My pa told me that in the years to come platooning will be a big part of the game."

"Platooning?" Seth asked.

"Yeah," the father said. "Lefties will face righties. Righties against lefties. And a player will be benched the rest of the time. But if yuh can switch hit, like my boy here, yuh got a better shot as a regular in the majors."

"Makes good sense to me," Seth admitted.

The father and the son crossed the road and the father fired up the truck.

Seth called out, "By the way, kid, what's you're name?"

But they couldn't hear him as they drove off.

Seth Lucas took the subway from New York to Brooklyn.

It was World Series time. The city of Brooklyn was excited, he couldn't help but notice as he took to the crowded streets closing in on Ebbets Field, the Brooklyn Dodgers home park. There, outside the booth, he purchased his bleacher ticket. People were chattering. *Could the Dodgers do it this year?* Hell, they had Duke Snider, Jackie Robinson, Roy Campanella, Gil Hodges, Pee Wee Reese. *Why wouldn't they do it?* The Dodgers had a good year in 1952, after the humiliating loss to the New York Giants in the 1951 National League playoff, in which Bobby Thomson hit a three-run homer off the Dodgers' Ralph Branca. In 1952 the Dodgers had won 96 games, had beaten the Giants to the National League pennant by four games, and were now facing the New York Yankees for the first game of the World Series at Ebbets Field, Seth's destination this afternoon.

Seth, too, was excited, for different reasons than most of the Brooklyn fans. He wanted to see the colored stars who had made it to the big leagues. Jackie Robinson, the first black to play big league ball in the twentieth century. There was also Joe Black and Roy Campanella, stars in their own right. And others were coming, he was told. Jim Gilliam from the farm team in Montreal. Don Newcombe, who was in military service. Seth felt proud of his race. Real proud.

At the same time he was disappointed that he didn't make it himself. That bothered him. . . now. . . as he nudged his way through the turnstile with his bleacher ticket. But Seth had not come to see only the black players. He had come to lay eyes on the Yankee center fielder he had been reading about in the papers for the last two years. The sportswriters said he was an Oklahoma kid. They called him the Commerce Comet. He was a blonde-haired boy, only twenty, coming on twenty-one. Seth was sure he was the miner's kid he remembered as a power-hitting thirteen-year-old on that makeshift field along Route 66 in Oklahoma seven years ago. In the 1952 regular season, the kid had hit a solid .311 with 23 homers and 87 runs batted in. Not bad for his second year in the majors. And he had replaced the retired Joe DiMaggio in the center field spot.

Seth took a seat near the bottom half of the bleacher section in center, where he wanted a good look at the action. The Yankees, who were the visitors, batted first. Seth sat up and stared at the kid when he came to the plate, third in the order, after Hank Bauer and Phil Rizzuto. Too far away to see really well, Seth nevertheless caught the same unchanged stance and left-handed swing as he faced Joe Black. The kid had made it, like he said he would. He was in the big leagues. And hot damn, playing for the mighty New York Yankees.

In the bottom of the inning, the kid ran out to his center field spot and turned around to face the plate. It had to be him, Seth concluded. Taller. More muscular. Body like a brick shithouse. Number 7. Only twenty years old.

It was him!

Seth waited outside the Yankees dressing room. A crowd of fans were also there, half of them kids. Each time the door opened and someone came out in a suit and tie, Seth noticed that it was quiet inside. No wonder. The Yankees had lost 4-2, although the kid had gone two-for-four at the plate. Both hits were singles. Then again, it was only the first game. The Yankees would come back. They always did in the important games. They had won the World Series three straight years, and were aiming for a fourth in 1952.

Then Seth saw the blonde-haired kid coming through the door in a suit, tie, and white shirt.

Seth charged to the front of the line.

"Hey!"

The kid stopped. "Hi. Want an autograph?"

It *was* him, Seth thought. Just more grown. The same boyish face, though.

"No. Not really. I came to say hi. Remember me?"

The player looked to be thinking hard, squinting his eyes. "Should I?"

"During the war in 1945, in Oklahoma. The summer. Our bus ran out of gas on Route 66 and your pa filled up his 50-gallon tank for us. I played shortstop out in the field. Yuh hit a few. Remember, now?"

The player smiled. "Yeah. Oh, yeah. It's good to see yuh again. I never did get your name."

They shook hands.

"We didn't get yours either. I'm Seth Lucas."

"Pleased to meet yuh, again, Seth."

"Good going, kid. You got a couple hits today off a pretty good pitcher."

"But we lost. Joe Black brought his stuff with him."

"You'll get them next game. So. . . I watched the papers. Yuh made it!"

The player cleared his throat. "Yeah. Thanks to my pa. You still playing?"

"Nope. Injured my knee bad in a collision at second making a double play back in 1947. My ball career is over."

"Too bad. Bum knee, eh? Tell me about it."

"Knee? You to?"

The player nodded. "Yeah."

"They got yuh playing center field. Yuh got a good arm out there. Real good."

"Thanks."

"Last time I remember you were an infielder. Yuh threw the ball all over the place."

The player laughed. "It never got better in the pros. Casey switched me to the outfield. Good thing he did, too."

"And now you're throwing strikes."

"What yuh doing, now?" the player asked.

"A job here and there as I work my way through university. Gotta get me an education."

The player smiled slowly. "That's smart," he uttered, not knowing what else to say.

"My pa said the same thing. By the way, how is *your* pa?"

The player hung his head for a moment and his eyes went glassy. "He died in May. It wasn't easy for him."

"Sorry to hear that." Seth paused. "He got yuh outta the mines, though."

The player looked straight ahead. "Yeah. Yeah, he did that, all right."

"And he was right about platooning. Stengel does it all the time, I see. Left-handed hitters against right-handed pitchers. . ."

"He sure as hell does."

Seth extended his hand. "I best be going," he said to the player, as they shook hands for the second and last time. "Good luck, kid."

"Thanks, Seth."

"I'll keep checking the papers, OK."

"OK. Sure yuh don't want an autograph?"

Seth chuckled. "Why not. It might be worth something one day."

"As my pa used to say, yuh never know. Here," the player said, "I got a note pad on me. Got a pen somebody?" He grabbed a pen from a nearby young boy and wrote down. . .

To my friend, Seth.

Yours truly, Mickey Mantle.

6

The Blizzard

The High Country through the mountain passes of New Mexico and Arizona were often hit with freak storms in the autumn and winter months. They called them Northers. Route 66 travelers in these areas had to be ready for such weather changes on a moment's notice.

SANTA ROSA, NEW MEXICO—NOVEMBER, 1951

The gas needle on Bruce Stockton's 1948 Buick sedan read *empty* this Friday morning, as the Standard Oil service station attendant ran out from the glassed-in office. Stockton remembered from past trips this way that it was the last stop for a good number of miles. Through the windshield, he saw that the blue western sky had some cloud build up. The day had been cool, only a few degrees above freezing. Typical for the season.

Stockton flipped the fedora back off his forehead and rolled down his window.

"Fill 'er up, please," he said to the young man.

"Yes, sir." The attendant touched the brim of his hat out of respect to the woman in the passenger seat. "Ma'am. Check the oil, too, sir?"

"No, thanks. I had someone look after it at the last place."

"I'll get to yer windshield."

"Thanks."

The attendant placed the gas nozzle into the tank and clicked it on

AUTO, then took his squeegee to the glass, cleaning it slowly without a single streak.

"There you go, sir," the attendant said at the open window. "Texas plates, huh?"

"That's right."

"Where yuh folks from?"

"Amarillo."

"Where yuh headed?"

"Gallup."

"Really. What yuh gonna do there?"

"Family wedding."

"You be careful out there. Suppose to be some bad weather moving into the west end of the state. Pretty high up in these parts. You may come into some snow or ice."

"Thanks. We'll be careful."

The attendant saw that the gas nozzle had stopped. "All done."

"How much do I owe you?"

The attendant glanced back at the numbers on the pump. "That'll be five dollars. . . and twenty cents."

Bruce whipped back his heavy coat, dug into his wallet, and paid the exact amount.

"Thank you, sir."

Bruce drove away and returned to Route 66, heading west. He gunned the V-8 motor and soon was up to sixty miles per hour.

"Did you hear that?" his wife, Angela, said.

"What?"

"Snow."

"Yeah, I heard," Bruce answered. "Big deal. We've driven in snow before."

"I don't like it."

"Don't worry about it. You wanna see your sister don't you, and the rest of the family?"

Angela dug her hands into the pockets of her winter coat and looked out the window at the scenery. Irritable all morning, she had been up with her husband since five. They had hit the road by six-thirty, hoping to make Gallup—450 miles away—by nightfall for the wedding the next day. Angela's baby sister, Lynn, the youngest of four, was finally getting hitched, to an oil man whose family had money. Early Friday was a good time to travel on Route 66. Before the weekend rush.

"How many more miles?" she snapped at her husband.

"To Gallup?"

"No, to Paris, France. What the hell did you think I meant?"

"OK, OK. Smart ass. Three hundred or so."

"I'm hungry," she barked.

"You are?"

"Yes, I am. Can we at least stop for breakfast somewhere?"

"Where?"

"I saw a diner across from the gas station back there."

"Why didn't you say so when I was filling up the tank?"

"You didn't ask me."

"Now I gotta turn around."

"So?"

"You always do stuff like that. You wait and wait!"

"What the hell's the matter? Will we lose too much time?"

"I told you to eat something at home before we left."

"Oh, sure. I was too busy packing for the two of us, while you were stuffing yourself in the kitchen. Besides, that was over three hours ago."

"All right, all right!"

Bruce slowed down and spun the car around. He raced to the diner and didn't say another word until he shut the motor off in a parking space alongside one of the large glass windows. "There."

"Thank you." She opened her door and waited. "Well, aren't you coming in?"

"Yeah, yeah."

Angela and Bruce were in trouble, on the verge of a divorce. In their early forties, married for eighteen years, they had basically grown tired of each other. It had started a good five years earlier. Life and marriage weren't fun any more. Both were restless. Bruce had worked too hard and was away too long, selling insurance—a tough sell at that—on the road. Angela raised the two twin girls—eighteen now—and kept the house in order. Then they began to snap at each other. They went out less. They made love a lot less. They avoided each other more. Once the girls were seventeen, Angela had to get out of the house during the day. She found a job. An attractive brunette still, men had always been interested in her. She had appeal. A secretary for an Amarillo real estate firm for the last year, many men had made a pass at her, especially one of the agents in the office. She gave in and had an affair. Then she quickly broke it off a month ago.

Bruce had three affairs in the last two years, as recently as three months back. Bruce and Angela finally had it out three weeks ago, when the kids were gone one evening. In a viscous argument, they both admitted being unfaithful. They had hardly spoken a word to each other since. For this car trip, they were now forced to interact. And they were also faced with a dilemma. How would they break it—a divorce—to the girls and the rest of the family? Perhaps the drive to Gallup would give them time to think. And plan strategy.

So they hoped.

Forty minutes later, the couple could see that the sky had clouded over.

"There's snowflakes in the air."

"Oh, come off it," Bruce laughed, behind the wheel. "You're seeing things." Then he finally saw them, too. They were light and powdery. "Hey, you're right," he admitted.

"What did I tell you. But. . . don't worry. . . we've *driven in snow before.*"

Bruce ignored her last remark, turned up the heat in the car, and clicked on the radio. He rotated the button from left to right. Hoping for a weather report from a local station somewhere, he received mostly static instead. Undoubtedly, a dead spot for radio signals.

They drove on. Bruce put his headlights and wipers on. Within an hour the flakes had grown larger and wetter. The road was now snow-covered and slippery. Traffic was down to forty miles per hour. Visibility at five hundred feet.

Another two miles. . . two hundred feet visibility.

Bruce remained about forty feet behind another car and just followed the red tail lights. They seemed to be the only two vehicles on the road heading west. In another five more minutes, they could barely even see the tail lights.

"Can you see?" Angela asked, gloom in her voice.

"Not really."

"What are we going to do?"

"I don't know. Keep going, I guess."

"Shouldn't we pull over somewhere?"

"Where?" he countered. "There's nothing out here."

"Pull off the road!" she pleaded.

"What the hell for?"

"Before we—"

"Oh, shit!"

Then they hit an icy patch and started to spin sideways. Before they knew it, they slid around five hundred and forty degrees and into the ditch, the front of the car coming to a stop and facing the other direction.

"Now look what you've done."

"Button it," Bruce replied.

"What now, oh bright one?"

"Shut up!"

Bruce could see that they had not gone all the way into the ditch and that it wouldn't be that hard to get out. "Get behind the wheel," he demanded. "When I pound on the back bumper, you slip it into first gear and give it gas. But not too much, OK?"

"OK."

"But for heaven's sake, when we get on the shoulder, stop there."

"No, I thought I'd drive onto the oncoming traffic."

"Quick with the smart cracks, aren't you?"

She stuck her tongue out at him.

Bruce got out of the car and slammed the door in anger. Angela moved over to the front seat. He slipped and slid around the side of the Buick as he positioned himself over the trunk. Ready, he banged on the bumper. She dutifully pressed the automatic transmission lever into first gear and pressed the accelerator. Bruce grunted and pushed. As he did that, she pressed even harder on the pedal. The back tires began to spin, the car raced forward several feet and Bruce fell flat on his face in the snow. Angela braked the car farther up the shoulder, and Bruce grabbed his fedora which had fallen to the ground. He ran up to the car, snow covering him from head to toe. When he opened the door, his wife turned to him and. . . burst out laughing.

"You did that on purpose!"

"Take it easy, Bruce." His anger only made her laugh all the more.

"I told you not to hit the gas too hard. OK, let me in!"

They returned to the road.

Another thirty minutes later, they saw a blinking orange neon through the blanket of heavy white snow. By then the storm had worsened, and Bruce was driving barely twenty miles per hour.

"Thank God," Bruce sighed. "Looks like a motel."

She grinned at him. "Don't tell me you're going to stop here? Why not keep driving?"

"Quiet." Ever so carefully, he steered off the slippery road and braked opposite the office. He shut the motor off. "Thank God, we made it."

"Where are we?"

"I don't know. Come on."

They went in, punched the bell at the front desk, and met a middle-aged woman in curlers coming through the doorway ahead.

"Howdy," she said. "Quite the storm were having."

The couple looked at each other. *Storm.* That was obvious.

"You're not kidding. Where are we?" Bruce asked.

"Just outside Pecos. I hope you're not planning on going anywhere."

"We did want to make Gallup by nightfall."

She shook her head. "Not a chance. They won't let yuh. I was just got off the phone with the highway patrol and they told me that Route 66 has been shut down all the way to the Arizona border."

"For how long?"

"Hard to know. They say this snow is going to keep up for the rest of today. Could be till early tomorrow or so by the time the ploughs get through and all."

The couple looked at each other again. The news hit them hard. Neither relished the idea of being stuck with each other for the next several hours, twiddling their thumbs.

Bruce shook his head. "What the hell are we going to do for a whole day?"

"You can always try out the hot springs," the woman replied with a wide smile.

Bruce fell asleep on the bed as soon as the couple made it to the motel room.

He woke up, leaned on one elbow, and saw that his wife was gone. He rose to his feet, slowly. He eyed his watch. An hour had passed. He remembered falling on the bed, coat, clothes and all, exhausted. He expected Angela to do the same. But it seemed she hadn't. At least, he couldn't remember that she had. He saw her suitcase on the floor. The bathroom door was open, no light on. *Where was she?*

He went to the window and peeked through the venetian blinds. The snow was still falling, visibility down to a hundred feet or less. *Where in tarnation was she?* Then, looking down, he saw fresh shoe prints in the snow, leaving the front door of their cabin. Her small steps. Size five. He had sudden visions of her lost and lying in the snow somewhere.

He threw his fedora and coat on, left the room, and followed the prints behind the cabin for more than two hundred feet until he came to the sign. . . HOT SPRINGS. *What was she doing out here, and all by herself?* He came to a rise, where he felt stone steps beneath the snow. He looked down. Size-five shoe. He could see that it was a steep hill. *Don't tell me she's taking the path to the springs?* Bruce shook his head and began to climb the stone path, not knowing what to expect.

After numerous steps, he now came to what appeared to be a road. And more stone steps along the shoulder on the other side. This road, too, was on an incline. He saw tire tracks as well as his wife's fresh prints. . . going up.

What was going on?

His curiosity getting the better of him, he continued on, taking the stones. Up he climbed. Then, ahead, he saw steam rising. The snow was still coming down. . . but melting before it hit the rocky ground. The air was warm. Walking on, he stopped. There. . . only a few feet away. . . was a large pool of water, twenty feet by twenty feet. And through the mist, he saw his wife—no one else—straight ahead in water up to her neck. She was leaning against a rock, eyes closed.

"Angela?"

She opened her eyes, then closed them. "Hi, there."

"So this is where you are," he said to her.

Angela opened her eyes again. For the first time in the day, she actually smiled in a way that appeared genuine. She was far from irritable now. "Decided to come up, did you?"

"Yeah. . . *well*.. I wondered what happened to you."

"I got tired of hearing you snore."

"That bad, huh?"

"Yeah. Concerned about me, were you?"

"Yes, I was."

She sighed. "Thanks. But you didn't have to be. I'm quite all right."

He shrugged. *What's with her?* he mused.

"This is so. . . so relaxing. The woman at the motel was right. It's fantastic. Like another world. Almost puts a different light on things, sort of."

Then Bruce thought of something. "Wait a second. I don't remember you. . ." He stopped, noticing her clothes on the rocks, near her. "Did. . . ah. . . you pack a bathing suit?" he said, stumbling with the right words to say.

"Nope."

"You sure?"

"Yeah, I'm sure."

"What are you wearing, then?"

"Nothing."

"Nothing!" he answered, startled, glancing over his shoulder. "You're out here all by yourself, buck naked! What if someone should come up?"

She laughed. "Yeah, in the middle of a snowstorm? Are you mad? We're the only two crazy enough to do that."

She stood up. She wasn't fooling. She was bare, buck naked. He nearly forgot how attractive she still was. And this after eighteen years of marriage and two kids who were born seven pounds each. "Come on in," she said, returning to the water, slowly, seductively. "It's kind of. . . like the first time we were in the shower together. Only, a lot more room."

"I'll say, it's a lot more room." Bruce remembered that time well. How could he forget? It was on their honeymoon in a Denver, Colorado hotel. "What's with you, anyway? You're not yourself."

"I'm not?"

"No."

"Never mind that. Take your clothes off. Come on in."

"Right here?"

"Why not?"

"Ah, what the hell. Nothing else to do."

"That's what I said."

"You did? To whom?"

"To myself, of course."

"All right, all right." He removed his hat, coat, shoes, socks, slacks, tie and shirt, and then his undershorts, then eased into the water, very slowly, sitting down near the edge.

"There you go," she said.

"Wow! This is. . . *ouch*, hot!"

"You'll get used to it, once you stay in a while." She advanced towards him. "Nice, eh?"

Bruce felt the sensation of the waters immediately. "Yeah, not bad, once you're in it."

"I told yuh so."

A change—a transformation—came over him. "Not bad at all."

"A little champagne would help, wouldn't it," Angela said. "Remember Denver?"

"I remember," Bruce replied, nodding, recalling the champagne drinking incident in the shower.

Water to her neck, Angela moved closer to him, slowly, and tucked her head under his arm. "Hi, there."

He looked down at her. "Hi."

They stared into each others eyes in a way that reminded them of their honeymoon and first few years of marriage. Then. . . it happened. By magic. Their lips met. Quick kisses at first. On the lips. On the neck. In the ears. On the ears. In seconds, they were carried away by the passion of it all. The kisses were longer and harder, searching each other's mouths. Neither one cared if anyone wandered by at this point.

To Bruce's surprise, Angela rose out of the water and straddled him. Then she boldly leaned back and wrapped her ankles around his neck, tickling his ears with her toes. Most of her body was out of the water. "We haven't done it this way in a while."

He chuckled. "I don't recall us ever doing it quite this way." Suddenly nervous, he glanced over his shoulder. "Geez, Angela. Here?"

"Relax. We're the only ones." She leaned forward, and slid her thighs into the water, grabbing for his fedora at the same time. Her breasts touched his face.

"Do you like that?" she purred.

"Yeah, I kinda do."

She grinned, plunking the fedora on his head. "There, you can leave your hat on."

"Thanks."

"Ride 'em, cowboy," she whispered into his ear, her voice soothing, as the snow fell.

Bruce found the whole thing difficult to believe at first. Was it really happening? The two of them hadn't been this relaxed, this happy together in a long time. Months. Years. He seemed to be in a magical fog, like the mist over the hot springs, as he and his wife got dressed and came down the path in the snow, hand in hand, to the motel room.

It didn't end there.

Angela hurried into the shower first, and he followed. She didn't mind. With the hot spray hitting them, he put his arms around her waist from behind.

"Hey, yuh, toots," he said, using the cute pet name that he hadn't used for years.

"Hey, handsome."

"Sorry, no champagne," he said, pressing his hands to her breasts.

She sighed, turned around and kissed him on the lips. "We won't be needing any. Not this time."

They jolted awake next morning when they heard a loud scraping coming from outside. The room was bright, light streaming through the venetian blinds.

"Hey," Angela said, rising. She strolled to the window, not a stitch on and peered around the side of the blinds. "It's a snow plough. It quit snowing. Hey, it's sunny out."

"Get back here," he said. "Somebody might see you."

She ran back, jumped under the covers, and snuggled up to her husband. "It's cold out there."

He checked his watch. "Holy smoke! It's ten o'clock!"

"Is it?"

"Come on, we got a wedding to go to!"

Gallup, New Mexico

The relatives at the reception couldn't help but notice the change in Angela and Bruce. Word had got out months ago that they were not getting along. Obviously, the stories weren't true. How could they be, seeing the two smiling at each other, dancing together, and holding hands. Many wondered who were the *real* newlyweds, them or the new couple.

After dancing two foxtrots in a row, Bruce left his wife at the table with her older sister, Cheryl, as he went to the bar. He sat on the stool and waited until the bartender approached.

"Another scotch-and-soda?" The black-tied bartender said. He was a trim man about forty, with a full head of dark hair.

"You remembered."

"You bet."

"Make it lighter than the last one. I better start winding down. It's getting late."

"Sure." The bartender mixed the drink in a clear glass and handed it to Bruce.

"Thanks."

"You're welcome." The bartender served another man on the stool to Bruce's left.

Bruce felt a tap on the shoulder. He spun around to see Vince, his brother-in-law, standing there with a drink in his hand, tie undone, shirt half-way out of his slacks. He had been drinking fairly heavily all night.

"What's up?"

"What's with you, anyway, pal?" Vince asked, sitting down on the stool quickly vacated by the other man.

"Huh?"

"What's with all the lovey-dovey stuff?"

Bruce smirked. "Yuh noticed?"

"*Yeah*, like. . . no kidding. I heard rumblings that you and Angela weren't getting along."

"Where'd yuh hear that?"

"A little birdie told me."

Bruce shrugged. "I thought we were through. Kaput! Until yesterday."

"Yesterday? What happened yesterday to change things?"

"I don't know, actually. It was on the way out here."

Vince laughed. "Get off it!"

"I'm not kidding, Vince."

"Well, fill me in."

"Can yuh keep a secret?"

"Cross my heart," he said, motioning with his finger across his chest.

"Promise you won't laugh?"

"I promise."

Bruce leaned closer. "Well, OK, you know when I was telling you that we had to stay over in the motel when the snow hit on Route 66?"

"Yeah."

"I didn't tell you about the hot springs."

"What hot springs?"

"Up the hill behind the motel. We just. . . I don't know how to describe it. We came together."

Vince frowned. "At the *hot springs*?"

"Yeah. That's what I'm telling you."

"It must be *some* water there. What was it, a fountain of youth?"

"You don't believe me, do you?"

"No, I suppose I don't."

"Don't knock it if you haven't tried it. The snow was coming down like mad. There we were. Stranded at a motel. Only one or two other rooms taken. At the springs. . . no one else around. Man, we were bare ass naked!"

"Hey, not so loud."

"Buck naked! We were like newlyweds, again. We made out. Right there!"

"Don't tell me, you did it?"

"Yep, right there."

"Geez. You did a dirty right there at the hot springs?"

"Then back at the motel. Twice."

"What are you two, a couple of sex machines?"

"We couldn't stop. It was like we were on our honeymoon all over again. You should go there some time, Vince. It might change your life. Who knows. Cheryl's, too."

Vince shrugged. "Maybe. You really think so?"

"Yeah, I do."

Vince shrugged again and left, while Bruce watched him return to his table. When Bruce looked back to the counter, the bartender was staring right at him.

"I couldn't help but overhearing," the bartender said, hands on the counter. "So, you've tried out the springs, have you?"

"I sure as hell did."

The bartender smiled. "Me, too," he said, while he fixed a vodka and orange juice for a customer. "It saved my marriage. Sounds like it did the same for you."

Bruce nodded. "I think it did. Thanks for the drink."

"You're welcome."

Armed with the drink, Bruce headed to his table, convinced that he and the bartender were on the same wavelength. *But I bet yuh he didn't do it with his hat on,* he thought.

7

An Evening to Remember

The Fifties saw the dawning of rock-n-roll, Marilyn Monroe, McCarthy-ism, the hula-hoop, the slinky, and. . . the drive-in theater. Route 66 had its share of the big screen, too. Teenagers flocked to the outdoor movies on the weekends once school was out. Little did some customers know that this particular drive-in night out would be like no other.

BETWEEN OKLAHOMA CITY AND TULSA, OKLAHOMA—JUNE, 1956

Terry Moore glanced in the rear view mirror, nervously adjusting it with his hand. He rubbed his eyes. He was bushed after driving most of the day. It was a hot Friday evening, unusually damp. The windows of the Desoto hardtop were down, creating a turbulence in the car. He observed his speedometer. Seventy miles per hour! Too fast. He let off until he was down to sixty. He didn't want to be yanked over by a Route 66 highway patrolman. Not now. Not when he was so close to the Missouri border.

He smiled for what was probably the tenth time in the last hour. Three hours to the border.

He still couldn't believe he had actually pulled it off. His glance at the briefcase on the floor in the front passenger side brought him back to reality, the evidence that it *was* true.

In the driveway between two houses, Bernie Clarke leaned over the fender of his 1936 Ford convertible hot rod. One foot on the running board and one hand on the carburetor linkage, he revved up the V-8 motor. His high performance carburetor—which he had installed the evening before—sounded tough. He opened the door, got in, and shut the motor off.

"Bernie!" his mother screamed out the open kitchen window.

"What?"

"How many times have I told you not to run your car so loud? It rattles the windows. . . *and* the television."

He shrugged. "OK."

His mother shook her head and went back to watch the six o'clock news.

Bernie folded his arms and looked around at the homegrown hot rod that he was so proud of. It blinked at him in the sunlight. Chrome everywhere. Bumpers. Engine. Door knobs. Already known for owning the fastest—and the cleanest—machine in town, Bernie had been seeing some stiff competition lately. The carburetor addition was perfect.

Nobody would touch him now.

At home, Grace Blanchard showered and threw on a pair of jeans and a clean blouse. In front of her bedroom mirror, she combed her hair. The weekend had arrived, and she was going out tonight with Bernie.

Mel Jordan took to the street and began to walk at his leisurely, confident pace, arms swinging. Known to friends by the nickname of Boomer (for how he hit opponents on the field), he was a hard-muscled kid, a linebacker on the school football team at Dryden High. And he had the typical solid, bulging neck to prove it. Few shirts could fit him in the collar. He preferred T-shirts, like the one he wore today. He had what many would call an overdeveloped body mixed with an underdeveloped brain. He was likeable, though. He must have done something right, his teachers had told him, because he was college-bound in the fall to Michigan Tech on a football scholarship.

Tonight he was going to walk his girl home.

After that. . . who knows?

Sandy Higgins finished serving a cold drink at the hamburger shop counter and turned to the wall clock behind her. *Almost there,* she sighed.

"Oh, miss," a man said to her across the counter. "Could I have some more coffee please?"

Sandy smiled as pleasantly as she could for one so anxious to end her shift. *Coffee on such a hot day,* she wanted to say. *Are you nuts?* "I'll be right with you."

Only ten minutes to go, she reminded herself, as she poured.

Bernie got into his best jeans and a clean t-shirt and picked up Grace at her house at the usual time of eight o'clock. As was her habit, she was already waiting on the front step. She could hear Bernie's noisy hot rod from a block away.

"Hi, baby."

Grace jumped in the front seat of the top-down convertible and slammed the door. "Hi. Muggy tonight."

"Yeah."

They were an attractive couple. He was a husky, dark-haired, crew-cut youngster who found his muscles lifting weights and playing sports. She was a pretty eighteen-year-old blonde, long-haired, long-legged, with olive skin—a freckle or two—who looked fabulous in her tight jeans and short-sleeved white blouse.

"It's OK with your parents?" he asked her.

"Oh, sure. But papa said you better have me home right after the last show. And he knows what time it ends."

"Geez, right after? There's no school anymore." He shrugged. "All right. Agreed."

"And if it starts raining, then you have to bring me home right away."

"Ah," he joked, "it's not going to rain."

"Pa says it might."

"So, what's playing?" he said, changing the subject.

"John Wayne movies. *Stagecoach* and *Rio Grande.*"

"Let's go, *pilgrim,*" he said, attempting an impersonation of the movie star that failed to impressed Grace.

"Droll," she said. "Very droll."

"I'll work on it."

"Don't give up your regular job."

Along the way to the drive-in, Bernie dropped in at his favorite hamburger shop, Stoley's. He parked outside.

"What are you doing?" Grace wanted to know. "Eating *before* the show?"

He shut the motor off. "Yeah. We got time. You want something?"

She grinned. "OK. Fries."

They ate quickly and were soon back on the road towards Route 66 and the drive-in, Grace's long hair swaying in the breeze. On a residential side street, heading out of town, Bernie saw one of his classmates with a young woman he didn't know, walking arm-in-arm on the sidewalk. He guided his car over to the curb beside the couple.

"Hey, Boomer," Bernie said. "What yuh doing?"

The couple hopped over to the car.

"Not much," Mel Jordan replied.

"Hi, there," Bernie said to the bright, skinny redhead in the waitress uniform.

"Hi," she replied in a high-pitched voice. She wasn't the prettiest female around, but she had an air about her that read *good time*.

"Didn't I see you earlier at Stoley's?"

"That's right," the girl said, her eyes admiring the hot rod. "Wow! I know who you are. You got the fastest car in town."

"That's what some say," Bernie answered proudly.

"Say hi to Sandy," Boomer said. "She finished up at Beckman High. This is Bernie and Grace. They went to Dryden, too. Bernie was the quarterback on the team."

"Hi, Sandy," Bernie and Grace said at the same time.

"Where yuh going?" Bernie asked.

"Walking Sandy home after work. She's just around the corner."

"What, no wheels?"

"Dad wouldn't let me have it tonight. He and mom were going out."

"Too bad."

"Them is the breaks."

"So, what yuh doing after?"

Boomer's eyes shot to his girlfriend, then back to Bernie. "Nothing that we know of."

"Wanna go to the drive-in? We got room. We got beer, too."

Boomer perked up. "Hmm. Really?" He glanced away, uncomfortably. "Well, I don't. . . you know," he said, stumbling with the right words.

Bernie understood. He had a summer job, manning the pumps at a local gas station. Boomer, on the other hand, was unemployed. "Don't worry. We'll get you in."

"Thanks, Bernie."

Grace knew what Bernie's raised eyebrows implied. "One of these times you're going to get caught," she said to him with a frown that developed into a sly smile.

"What do yuh say?" Boomer turned to Sandy.

"A sneak-in, eh?"

"Yep."

"Swell," she answered immediately. "But I think I better change."

"Hop in," Bernie said. "We'll drive yuh over. Where yuh live?"

"Up the street. Hang a left two blocks up," Sandy said. "Hey, can you lay rubber with this thing?"

"You kidding me?"

The couple climbed into the back seat. Bernie glanced over his shoulder, revved the motor up, dropped the clutch, and smoked his tires for a good thirty feet.

Bernie braked his hot rod over to the shoulder, a mile away from the drive-in, visible up the country road just off Route 66. On the western horizon, the sun's last rays of the day were poking through the cloud cover.

"OK," he said to Boomer and Sandy in the back seat. "Show time. In the trunk, you two."

When Boomer and Sandy squeezed out of the car, Boomer's attention turned to the sky. "I don't like this."

"What?"

"The clouds. We're going to get some rain."

"Not you, too." Bernie unlocked the trunk and flipped it up. "Get in," he said. "But I'll put the top up, though, just in case."

Outside Tulsa

Terry Moore stared out his passenger window at the darkening sky to the southwest. He saw the high cumulus clouds. They were white and puffy. Rain was coming. Perhaps a storm, with that anvil cloud to the west. As sure as God made little green apples. He yawned twice in under a minute. He couldn't take it any longer. He had almost driven off the road twice already because he was so tired. He had better hold up for a spell. Ten minutes. . . then he'd go the rest of the way. Non stop.

He slowed down and turned onto the shoulder, near an underpass ahead. In another minute, he was fast asleep.

Bernie turned into the drive-in gravel road and hit a wide bump.

"Ouch!" Sandy screamed from the trunk.

"Quiet!" Bernie barked. "We're almost there."

Boomer had his arms around Sandy in the totally-dark trunk. "Shush," he said to her.

"That hurt," she pouted. "How can anybody hear anything with those mufflers, anyway?"

In a short time, the hot rod had stopped. Boomer and Sandy heard a woman's voice from above.

"Hello, there."

"Hi," Bernie replied.

"Two?"

"Yes, ma'am."

"Any alcohol?"

"No, ma'am," Bernie lied. It was in the trunk beside Boomer's legs.

"Anybody in the trunk."

"You kidding," Bernie said, quickly. "It's too small."

"Yeah, I guess it is."

"I think I have to sneeze," Boomer whispered.

"Oh, no."

"Just kidding."

Outside, the voices continued.

"That'll be four dollars."

"Yes, ma'am."

Bernie drove the car through the gate and headed straight for the back row. He waited a few more minutes until it grew darker, then let Boomer and Sandy out. Boomer had the case of beer with him. They were soon popping the tops inside the top-up convertible.

"Getting a little cooler all of a sudden, isn't it," Grace said.

"Yeah," Bernie replied. "It sure is." He rolled his window up until there was a one-inch space at the top.

After two beers, Bernie left for the restroom. When he came out, he saw that it was beginning to rain. Lightly, at first. Then a little harder. And finally a near downpour. All in the space of less than a minute. Grace's father was right about the weather. There goes the Friday night fun. The screen was still playing *Stagecoach*, the first movie. Maybe the rain would stop, he hoped. But the pelting of hailstones made him changed his mind.

Then it hit with a vengeance.

Before turning in the direction of the car, he heard a sound like a locomotive, mixed with a scream and an eerie whine. He stopped and looked to the darkened sky. A flash of lightning brightened an area on the ground measuring at least a mile across. For a split second, it seemed to be daylight. The sound meant only one thing. He couldn't see it, but he could hear it.

It was a twister. A night twister. The worst kind!

Moore heard the same noise. He had never been this close to a tornado before, and he did the only thing he could do. The brightly-lit drive-in up the road was too far away. Dark now, he flicked the headlights on to shine on the road ahead, grabbed his briefcase, and ran for the safety of the underpass. He had never been so scared in his life. The tornado had to be very near now because the wind had picked up to where it had to be well over eighty miles per hour.

The noise grew closer. . . and louder.

The winds picked up even more. Thunder overhead pounded the ground beneath him. Moore tucked himself under the bridge and clung to the concrete post, his right hand through the briefcase. The tornado was so close now that it had flattened out the weeds. The sound was vibrating his ears. *Louder. . . closer* it came. Until it was right overtop him.

He tried to hang on to the post. . . but it was no use. It was pulling him away.

He screamed into the night. But no one heard him.

* * * *

At the drive-in, Bernie ran for the car. The other three met him half-way before he could get there.

"What should we do?" Grace yelled, over the roar.

Bernie glanced around. The car? No way. "The snack counter! Come on!"

It was raining much harder now, the pellets bigger, almost hurting. The two couples ran for cover, and squeezed through the doorway with a handful of other people, just as the windows blew out and the roof started to groan above them.

Then the lights flicked out.

"Get face down!" Bernie yelled, throwing himself over the frightened Grace, taking her to the floor with him. Boomer did the same to protect Sandy. "Cover up the back of your heads."

Dust and splinters flew about. The roof banged. . . buffeted. . . banged again. . . then twisted off as if a giant cut it away with a large can opener. Lightning cracked overtop. The roar, by now, was too deafening to speak. To top it off, a deluge of rain descended on them.

Then. . . it was over as quickly as it hit. The rain, the sound, the wind all died down.

Bernie got to his knees in the darkness, helping Grace. They looked up at the same time. They stared at each other for several long seconds, as Boomer and Sandy stirred beside them. Did it really happen? So fast?

"You guys OK," Boomer asked his friends, rising, helping Sandy up.

"We're still here," Bernie replied. "I can't believe the walls stayed up. Let's go see what the rest of the place looks like."

Outside, under the full moon, they stood in shock. More than half the cars had vanished from their parking spots. But they saw that Bernie's car remained. Bernie grabbed Grace by the hand and sauntered over to it.

"What's this?" Grace asked.

"What?"

"On the ground."

They stopped to bend down. Boomer and Sandy ran to them. They noticed it, too. Money! All over the wet ground. Hundreds of paper bills.

"Geez," Boomer said. "Twenty. . . and fifty dollar bills."

"Oh, yeah? Well, I got a hundred!"

"Get off it." Boomer snatched the bill from Sandy's hand. It was true. A *hundred dollar bill.*

"There's more!" Grace yelled, scooping the bills off the ground. "They're all in fifties and hundreds!"

"Wait a minute," Boomer said to Bernie. "We can't take it. That has to be the snack counter money."

"In fifties and hundreds? You crazy? They don't handle that kind of money," Bernie said, reaching for his share of the bills, crunching them together in his hands to make room for more.

"Where did it come from then?"

"Hell if I know. It's every man. . . and woman for themselves."

Grabbing all they could in their fists before too many other people had caught on to what was happening, the two couples jumped into Bernie's hot rod.

They raced out of the drive-in, flying past several damaged telephone poles.

At a coffee shop booth in town, they discussed their situation.

"We should have stuck around to help, don't you think?" Grace said.

"Help? How? Clean up?" Bernie answered her. "What could we have done?"

"Still."

"Anyway, look, we all agree we share the money four ways," Bernie said, lowering his voice.

The other three nodded, reluctantly.

"How much did you say we found altogether?" Bernie asked Boomer.

"Four thousand and two hundred."

"That's one thousand and fifty each."

The other three nodded as a group once more.

Grace glanced over her shoulder to make sure no one else was listening. "Don't you just wonder, though, where the money came from?"

"Yeah, it obviously came from somewhere," Sandy said. "It's not really ours."

"Who says?" Boomer barked.

"Atta boy," Bernie said, slapping his friend on the shoulder. "We weren't the only ones picking up the dough. Anyway, this is what we do. Split our shares. Lie low for a while. And don't tell a soul."

"Where are we going to hide a thousand dollars cash?" Boomer asked.

"That's up to each of us. After a few weeks, we spend it. A little bit at a time." He looked around the booth. "Very little, OK? Well?"

"OK, OK," Grace replied.

Boomer nodded. "All right." He turned to his girlfriend.

"OK," Sandy sighed, heavily. "I'm not going to be left out."

"What are you going to do with your share?" Boomer asked Bernie.

Bernie shrugged. "Actually, I never thought of it till now. Maybe, some speed parts for the rod. It could use a new hot camshaft."

"Clothes for me," Grace said.

"You will," Bernie chuckled. "What about you, Sandy?"

"Clothes for me, too," she said.

"Boomer?" Bernie asked.

"Well, with college coming up, I'll find some use for it."

The next morning, Bernie woke up to his mother calling him from the bottom of the stairs.

"Bernie!"

Bernie stumbled out of bed in his undershorts. At the open door, he poked his head around the corner. "What?"

"Come down here."

"What for?" he grumbled.

"Someone wants to talk to you."

"Who?"

"Come down and see. Now! Get dressed first."

Bernie put on a wrinkled t-shirt and jeans and descended the stairs to find two big uniformed policemen at the door with his parents.

"Bernie Clarke?" one of the policemen asked, with authority.

Bernie's father suddenly appeared from around the corner.

Bernie swallowed. "That's me."

"Someone saw your car racing away from the drive-in last night."

"Yeah. . . so?"

"Why so fast?"

"We were there when the twister hit. Why shouldn't we leave? There was nothing to stick around for. At least we had a car to leave in. Some of them didn't. Is there a crime in leaving a drive-in?"

"Don't get sassy, boy," Bernie's father said to his son.

"What I wanted to say," the policeman continued, "was someone saw you picking up money off the ground, then leaving with three others in your car. Although the electricity was out and it was pitch dark, your car was still easily identifiable."

"Money!" Bernie's mother said. "What money!"

"You'll find out soon enough, ma'am. What we want is the cash, son. Give it to us now and you will not be prosecuted. You have our word on that." The other policeman nodded. "Too many of you were doing the same thing to arrest anybody. So, just give us the money. It's not yours. You have no right to it."

Bernie grunted, shaking his head. "I knew it was too good to be true."

"By the way, how much did you make off with?"

"Four thousand and two hundred dollars," Bernie answered the policeman. "We split it four ways."

Bernie's father groaned.

His mother began to cry. "Oh, Bernie!"

"We want to know who the other three people were in your car, too. We want their names and addresses, son. But we want your money first."

Bernie glanced over at his parents. It was no use. "OK."

The next afternoon Bernie was sitting on the front steps of his parents house when the wrapped-up newspaper was thrown into the yard by the paper boy. Bernie undid the bundle. The front page headline jumped out at him.

TWIN TWISTERS HIT

Bernie read the article from start to finish. Two twisters had hit at the same time, a mile apart. Both had remained on the ground in the Tulsa outskirts for about sixteen minutes. The city was missed entirely. The twisters had hit the drive-in, killing four, injuring twelve. Ten cars were written off. Hailstones the size of golf balls were reported. Bernie's hot rod had the dents to prove it. Those who had been in the drive-in were interviewed and recalled hearing a grinding, whistling sound as the twister drew near.

Then Bernie saw another bold headline on the front page, off to the left.

TWISTER ENDS ROBBER'S LIFE

Bernie read with interest. There had been a bank robbery in Oklahoma City. A theft of $40,000 dollars in bills of twenties, fifties, and hundreds. The robber then escaped east down Route 66 towards Missouri. But never made it. The tornado hit when the robber had neared the drive-in. According to a bank clerk at the Oklahoma City bank, the robber had stuffed the money in a briefcase. Apparently, the money blew out. Some of the bills landed inside the drive-in grounds. The rest had scattered across several hundred feet of bald prairie. The robber was discovered a mile away. Dead. Most of the money had been recovered. The briefcase itself was yet to be found.

Maybe it was somewhere over the line in Missouri, Bernie smirked to himself.

You might even say. . . the briefcase was still at large.

8

Through These Eyes

We all have talents. Most are of the basic variety. Some more unusual than others. One young lady, out on her own for the first time in her life, had a talent—more like a curse—and it scared her.

Amarillo, Texas—Summer, 1960

She packed her suitcase in her bedroom as quietly as she could this early Saturday morning. She checked her wrist watch and left the written note to her mother on the bed. At ten minutes to seven, her fifteen-year-old brother and her mother were probably still dead-to-the-world asleep. She quietly tip-toed down the stairs to the hall, suitcase in hand, and out the door into the bright sunshine. She removed the sunglasses from her blouse pocket and flipped them on. Then she snatched one last, longing look at the two-story house inside the picket fence. Was she doing the right thing? Sure, she was. She quickly broke into a brisk walk on the quiet street. The note she left would tell it all.

She hoped.

Rita had done everything she could think of, carefully and method-ically. She had gotten all her own washing finished the night before. In the afternoon, she had taken out two hundred dollars in travelers checks at the bank and told the manager that she would arrange to have the rest of her account—almost a thousand dollars—sent by wire once the manager had heard from her. She told only one person, her friend,

Gail, what she was up to. Gail swore she wouldn't tell anybody until her friend was well on her way down the road on Route 66.

Rita Sperry was a dimpled, twenty-year-old brunette, whose bangs made her appear younger. Some admirers considered her beautiful, although she never rated herself in such a way. She was a slim woman with a shapely figure, and fine features. She had boyfriends, none of them serious relationships, though. Two of them felt differently. But she didn't share their feelings. She had finished high school the spring of 1959 and had worked for a solid year. Living at home, she saved money. With no one or nothing to keep her in Amarillo, she felt that now was the time to leave. Her widowed mom would have to understand. Start new. Go west. Far west. Far away from Amarillo. Never before had she ventured outside her home state. That would soon change.

Rita suddenly stopped walking and thought of her mom. She could imagine her in her bedroom, sleeping soundly. Should she run back and let her mom know? Rita took up the walk again. No, she couldn't. No way! Her mom would try to talk her out of going. She'd cry. She'd plead. Rita didn't want tears. She was a responsible young lady now, out on her own. She remembered how her mom cried at her dad's funeral in December. Rita had warned her dad not to drive out in that ice storm that clobbered the Texas Panhandle two days before Christmas. But he had to go visit his sick sister at Claremore. While she had begged him to stay home, she could actually see her dad spinning off the road and overturning his car in the ditch.

"Don't worry, kiddo," he had said to her on the porch. "I'll be back tomorrow."

"But, dad, don't. Don't go, please."

"Hush, now. You take care of your brother and your mama. I'll be home for supper."

He never made it.

Rita walked even faster. At the end of the block, she crossed the street. She pictured a semi stopping on the highway, a young man inside. *T-shirt, muscles, and ball cap.* That was something to smile about.

Was it finally the man she was waiting so long for? All the more reason to leave.

* * * *

The semi driver slowed down his westbound rig once he hit the Amarillo city limits on Route 66. Coming through this way many times before, he knew the cops would often come out of nowhere and issue speeding tickets to those out-of-town culprits who chose not to back off the pedal.

He was quickly in the middle of restaurants, bookstores, antique shops, and a gas station on a corner. Then. . . within a short time, he was back in the country again. Before he could wind up the rig into the next gear, he saw a dark-haired young woman on the side of the road with a sign that read CALIFORNIA. He touched the brakes and threw the wheel over to the right. He watched in the large side mirror with the diesel engine idling. The woman ran towards him.

He politely leaned over and opened the door for her. "Hi," he said, staring down at the brunette in sunglasses, jeans and white blouse.

"Going my way?"

"You bet. Hop in."

Rita threw the California sign inside the suitcase, clipped it back up, and climbed up onto the metal ramp. "Thanks."

She dropped the suitcase on the wide floorboards in the cabin, and placed her feet on top. She smiled over at the handsome man in the New York Yankee baseball cap, three or four years older than her. *It was him. T-shirt and muscles. Baseball cap.* She watched as he banged the big rig into first gear and steered onto Route 66, winding the rig up once again. He seemed a nice enough sort. Friendly smile, clean-shaven, and richly tanned.

"Traveling all by yerself, are yuh?" the driver asked.

"Yeah," she replied, shyly.

"You're up early."

"Yes, I am."

"Where yuh going?"

"California."

"I see that. Whereabouts in California?"

"Los Angeles, maybe."

"You don't know?"

She shrugged. "Not really."

"You're in luck. I'm going right into LA, if you happen to be going that way. Moving a family from Chicago. Seems a lot of people are heading to California."

"That's what I've heard."

"What are you going to do there?"

"I don't know yet. Work. Start a new life. Any place is better than Amarillo."

He smiled. "I'm Brett Conway."

She turned to him, taking her sunglasses off. "Rita Sperry."

"Nice to make your acquaintance, Rita."

"Same here. Drive moving trucks, do yuh?"

"Yep. Eastern Movers. Biggest in the country."

"How long you been doing this?"

"Close to five years now. I've seen almost every state in the union."

"Must be nice to travel, seeing all those places."

"Yeah, it is," he grinned, glancing at her.

"What's the nicest place you've been?"

"California," he answered quickly. "So, what did you do in Amarillo?"

"Not much."

"Did yuh work?"

She grunted. "Yeah. Sold whatever boring items people want to buy at a hardware store."

Brett smiled and turned his attention to the road. "Looks like a great day out there."

"Yeah, sure does," Rita said, thinking that her mom must have found the note by now.

"Geez, this country could use some rain. Kind of on the dry side."

"It's normal this time of year. You get used to it."

"Have yuh had something to eat?"

"I skipped breakfast this morning." Didn't have time, she wanted to say instead.

"That's not good to skip breakfast," he scolded her in a cheerful manner. "There's a diner this side of Route 66 at Vega that serves the best meals around."

"Sounds swell to me," Rita answered, with a passion.

"Good. We'll stop there. Mind if I smoke?" Brett asked.

"Go ahead. It's your truck."

"Not mine. . . really. . . the company's."

Rita glanced out the window.

She was leaving Texas. Her home state. Born and raised. She thought of her friend, Gail, then turned and said to Brett, "How many times have you been to California?"

"Three, no, four times," he told her.

"What's it like?"

"Ah," he sighed, a glint in his eye. "Once you hit the coast, it's the best weather around. Lots of sunshine. Never gets that hot, though. Palm trees. Sand. Beaches. Orange groves. You'll love it."

"I sure hope so."

Following a breakfast of bacon and eggs, toast, orange juice and coffee outside Vega, Rita and Brett returned to the road. More cars and trucks were moving both ways. The weekend traffic was starting. It would be busy for a couple days now.

They crossed into New Mexico.

"You ate pretty good back there."

Rita smiled, her dimples forming. "Yeah, I did, didn't I." She folded her arms. "Do you travel Route 66 a lot?"

"Yeah, I do," Brett replied. "She's a pretty good road. Kind of slow at times. That'll be fixed sometime in the future."

"How?"

"Don't yuh know what the latest gab is?"

"About what?"

"Route 66. I read this newspaper article back east that says the feds in Washington are funding a new road system, clear across the country. Route 66 will be put out to pasture."

"Really," Rita replied, only partly interested.

"Interstates, they call them. Four-lane highways. No stop-and-go through towns and cities. No sir, nothing like that. I can high-ball it all the way!" he said, excited. "I could cut a day or two off traveling time between Chicago and LA." Then Brett calmed down. "But, from what I heard, it won't be for a while. So, why hold your breath, eh? I'll be retired or get out of trucking by the time they kill ol' Route 66 for good."

"Yeah. It probably will take a while, for sure." The only thing that Rita cared about was that Route 66 was her getaway.

Then, without warning, a vision began to come to her. So fast and

105

furious that she sat up and gasped softly. Goose bumps broke out on her arms.

Brett glanced over, seeing her stare straight ahead at the open road as if in a trance. "Anything wrong?" he asked. "You look like you've seen a ghost."

Rita composed herself. "Oh. . . nothing. Just something. . . in my throat." She faked a cough.

The two grew quiet.

Rita leaned her head against the half-open passenger window. She closed her eyes. She was tired after all, she quickly realized, although she'd had nine hours of sleep the night before. Perhaps, it was the drone of the engine that was doing it. There, in a semi-conscious state, the vision came again. Slowly, but as clear as a movie on a screen. She saw it all in living color. It was a rocky scene. Dry country. The sun was setting over three jagged peaks in the distance. There was a bend in the road. It was a bad accident. There was smoke and flames. Several cars were smashed together into a conglomeration of heated metal. A Hot Zone. Five cars along with two half-ton trucks. Other cars were stopping along the shoulder, near a dried-out creek bed.

People were getting out. Another of the smashed vehicles was a semi, like Brett's. It lay, tipped-over and sideways in a ditch near a New Mexico Route 66 sign. People were running up to it. A young man was inside, not moving, crunched in the corner of the cabin. Blood covered his face and chest. Glass was strewn all about from the punched-in windshield. On the other side of the windshield—on the ground—was a bruised and bloody woman, face down, in jeans and a white blouse. She wasn't moving.

Then she saw the two words in white bold lettering on the side of the door. . . EASTERN MOVERS.

She came to with a jump and a scream that startled Brett.

"Geez, don't do that!"

"Stop the truck!"

"What for?"

"Stop it!"

"OK!" he yelled. "OK!"

She turned to him, as he hissed the truck to a stop. She moved closer and wrapped her arm around his bicep.

Brett didn't know what to think. "What's with you, anyway? You're getting pretty serious," he kidded her. "And we haven't had a date yet."

She looked up at him. "I don't want to lose you."

"You wanted me to stop the truck so you could tell me that?"

"It took me so long to find you."

"What are you talking about?"

She squeezed his bicep tighter. "You must be confused."

"You bet the hell I am."

She pulled away and jammed herself on the passenger side of the cabin. "I'm sorry for being so. . . so forward."

"I didn't mind," he said, slowly. "Really I didn't. But what's this about not losing me?"

"I've had visions about you for two years. In a t-shirt and muscles. And your ball cap."

"Interesting. Do you have these visions often?"

"You sound like a doctor. Yes, I have them two or three times a week. Sometimes more. I see things before they happen."

Brett cleared his throat. "Oh. You see the future with these visions, do you?"

"Yes."

"So. . . OK. . . who's going to win the World Series this year?"

Rita chuckled. "It's not like that. I couldn't tell you that, unless I get a vision about it. I don't have a crystal ball. I usually see disasters, just before they happen."

"Hmm," he grunted.

"You don't believe me."

"I can't say I do."

"I saw my father's car accident before he left the house. I tried to warn him."

"And?"

"It was no use."

"Any other times?"

"I once saw a three-car accident in Amarillo. I was sitting on the front porch. I could picture the whole thing. Then an hour later I heard about it on the radio."

"It sounds kind of far-fetched to me."

"Just this morning when I left the house I had another vision. You were driving a semi. You were wearing a t-shirt. You had muscles. You had a baseball cap. You're the one."

Brett's face showed it all. "Me," he said matter-of-factly.

"Yes, you."

Brett couldn't come up with anything to say for several long seconds. "You're pretty and all, but just like that, huh?" He snapped his fingers. "I'm the man of your dreams. Is that what you're saying?"

"Yes," she said, with conviction.

"Don't I have any say in this?"

Rita couldn't answer that.

"How do you know I'm not attached?"

"OK. Are you seeing someone?" Rita probed.

"No. My girlfriend and I broke up last week. But that's beside the point."

"Like I said, I'm sorry for being so forward." Her voice turned to near-anger. "Look, I'm tired. I better let you drive. We have a long way to go." Her eyes became glassy, as she studied him. "I promise I won't bother you. I could use some sleep."

Brett rolled his eyes, hit the signal bar and turned the rig back onto the highway.

Rita opened her eyes slowly and rubbed them. She felt the drone of the semi engine and the rumble of the road beneath her. She took a breath, sat up, and looked around. Her head was sore from her slouched position against the passenger window. She saw that the landscape had changed. It was rocky, and much drier. And she thought Texas was dry. The road was busy with weekend vehicles. Her eyes rested on the horizon ahead. There they were! The same three peaks in the vision.

"How's the sleeping beauty?" Brett asked.

She cleared her throat. "Not that good." She eyed her watch. She had been out for more than two hours.

"What do you mean not that good? You look a little spooked, again," he said.

Her eyes were on fire. "Brett?"

"Yeah?"

"I saw a vision before I fell asleep."

"Not again."

"Listen to me," she blurted. "I saw three peaks, the same ones as out there." She pointed at the spot through the windshield.

"So?"

"Please! Don't. . . don't go any further."

"Why not?"

"Get off Route 66. Take another way."

"Come off it! I can't do that!"

"There's an accident coming. You're going to be in it. We both will be. Get off the road! NOW! It's coming!"

"OK. That's it. Out you go. You scare me. There's a motel and gas station up ahead."

Rita fell silent.

Brett drove on and stopped the rig on the shoulder fifty feet from the gas station entrance. He leaned across Rita's lap and opened the door for her. "There. This is where you're getting off."

Rita didn't move. She stared at Brett with puppy-dog eyes. "Don't go any further. Please, Brett, don't."

"Cut it out!" He was yelling now.

"I'm trying to warn you."

"Get out!" he repeated.

Frustrated, she got down onto the ramp, clutching her suitcase, and leaped to the gravel shoulder.

"Good-bye," he said to her, then banged the passenger door closed. "Good riddance."

"So long," she said quietly to herself as Brett pulled away.

She watched as the rig drove out of sight over a rise a half-mile away. Off to the left, two or three miles across the sand and sparse vegetation, was a small town, a few buildings. She glanced around at her immediate surroundings. At least there was some civilization, out here in the middle of nowhere. She dragged her suitcase to the adobe-style motel office beside the gas station. She could see only one car. Outside on the boardwalk was a woman in a peach-colored dress, watering potted plants hanging from the porch. She had been watching from the time Brett dropped Rita off. As Rita neared, the woman straightened up. She was about forty-five, plump, her face baked from the sun. She had a mix of the dark Navajo-Hispanic features. Rich golden skin. High cheek bones.

"Good morning," she said, followed by a friendly smile. "Welcome to the Santa Mino."

Rita wiped her forehead with her hand. It was getting warm. "Morning."

"Hitch-hiking, are yuh?" The woman set her watering can down.

"Yeah," Rita replied, looking to the road west.

"Where yuh headed?"

"California."

The woman seemed to expect the answer. "So's a lot of other people."

"Would you happen to have any ice water? I'm dying of thirst."

"Coming right up," the woman said. "Come on in."

Rita sat on a couch in the lobby, drinking from her tumbler, while the woman went on with her watering. Rita glanced out to the busy road. Cars whistled by in both directions. She leaned her head on the back of the couch, staring at the ceiling. She did the right thing, she rationalized in her mind. She got off the truck. She had to look after herself. At least she had warned Brett. She would never see him again. She was certain of that.

But why the vision of him in the first place?

The woman came in. "Did that hit the spot?"

"On the button. Thanks."

"You're welcome." The woman took the empty tumbler from Rita's outstretched hand. "You look troubled."

"Men," Rita replied.

The woman chuckled. "Don't I know it, honey."

The wall phone rang with a loud shrill. The woman walked over and answered.

"Santa Mino." The woman paused to listen. "Hi, Magen." Another pause. "You're kidding. That's awful." She listened longer, then said, "OK, I will." The woman clicked the receiver in place and frowned. "It appears your trucker friend drove into an accident."

Rita gasped.

"Down the road," the woman replied. "About five miles. Several cars and trucks. Both sides of the road are blocked. I'm going to draw up a sign and let drivers know to turn back. This will tie up Route 66 for hours." The woman walked off, leaving Rita alone.

Rita sat down, hands over her eyes. She wanted the tears to come, but they wouldn't, for some strange reason. She thought of many things. Her bizarre visions. Why? Why was she getting them? She thought of her mom. Her dad. Her brother. Brett. Heavy in thought, she failed to see or hear the truck slowly advancing on the station and parking off to the side.

But she did hear the footsteps on the boardwalk. She looked up.

"Hi, Rita."

It was Brett, standing in the doorway.

"Is it really you?"

He grinned at her. "It's me."

"You're alive." She stood up slowly, then ran to him.

They embraced, then she kissed him on the mouth with a passion that surprised even her. Brett's powerful arms locked her to him.

Her face in his chest, she said, catching her breath, "You came back." She gazed into his eyes. "Why?"

"At the last minute, I stopped and pulled over to the side for a few minutes to think about what you said. A mile up the road, I saw the accident. Smoke and flames. You were right. Then I turned around and came back for you."

"I'm so glad."

"I'm sorry for yelling at you."

"You're forgiven."

"Thank you for saving my life."

Rita closed her eyes. Finally, someone had listened to her warnings. "You're welcome."

"Will you give me a second chance to be the man of your dreams?"

"Of course. Brett?"

"Yeah?"

"Do you know a detour out of here?"

"I'll find one." He kissed her lightly on the lips. "Let's go."

They walked out, hand-in-hand, to the semi. Brett moved the rig east on Route 66.

Rita's visions stopped for good that afternoon.

9

The Phantom

Fast cars were an instant hit, a way to go for youngsters in the 1950s and early 1960s. It was the era of hotrods, roadsters, Corvettes, and T-Birds, before the pollution-control devices and expensive fuel came along in the late '60s to spoil everybody's fun.

PHOENIX, ARIZONA—SEPTEMBER, 1962

Mechanic Jimmie Whitman felt like a king the day he drove his brand new, candle-apple-red 1962 Chevy Corvette with the removable hard-top roof off the car lot. He had arrived. *A Corvette.* He had paid for a quarter of it up front, the rest on a bank loan. *Why not treat himself?* He had a good job with a Chevy dealership in town. Besides, he got a deal on it.

The first place he drove his shiny sports car—top off—was to his friend's house in the east end. Bud Palmer was puttering around in his garage. He and Whitman had met in high school and had a mutual love of cars. . . and girls.

"Wow!" Palmer mustered, coming down the driveway, whistling. "You did it."

"Yeah." Whitman smiled, standing over his new purchase with his friend, as the Corvette idled.

"I'm jealous," Palmer said. "Only single men can afford one of these things."

Whitman laughed. "I thought I'd better grab one before Linda. . . well. . . you know."

"Yeah," Palmer grunted. "You don't have to tell me. So when are you two getting hitched?"

"When I ask her, I guess. It could be soon."

"How soon?"

"I'll let you know."

Palmer turned his attention once more to the Corvette. "So, did yuh get the Ramjet fuel-injected model?"

"Yeah, with the 327."

"Four-on-the-floor."

"The only way to go."

"Sounds like a pretty tough cam in it. How much horsepower?"

"Three hundred and sixty."

"Ooh. Nasty shit, there, pal," Palmer grinned. "You gonna take me for a spin?"

"What are we waiting for? Get in. I won't honk on it too much, though. I still have to break her in."

"Understandable."

"By the way, I'm going cruising tonight. Out there with the big boys. Linda can't make it. Wanna come?"

"I'd love to. But I promised the wife I'd take her to *West Side Story*. Sorry."

"OK. I'll just have to go on my own, then."

Flagstaff, Arizona

At nightfall, Warren Griffey hopped into his shiny, pale-green 1932 Ford roadster minus the fenders and headed west on Route 66 to Karen's Diner at the edge of town. As he chugged into the parking lot, he saw heads turn on the other side of the windows inside the building. Every time he came through he always rattled the glass.

This was where the boys with the hot cars hung out. Carl Garrison's 1962 Chevy Impala, Rick Robinson's 1955 T-Bird, and Kevin Leacy's 1956 Crown Victoria were all parked together outside. All three cars were tough and fast. But Griffey could beat them all because he had the meanest machine in and around Flagstaff. His homegrown hotrod with the suicide doors sported a 409 big block Chevy motor capable of over four-hundred horsepower. It had a distinct, beefy pitch to it when the four-barrel carb cut in at the high RPMs. "Just some fine tuning," Griffey would say.

Before Griffey could jump out, Leacy, Robinson, and Garrison crowded up to him in the lot. Griffey was somewhat of a legend. A high school dropout, a job drifter, all he had was his car and his occasional girlfriend, Bonnie. He was twenty-two with no real future. Someone once called him an "escapee from the fifties." He played the part with his greasy, black hair, leather jacket, and toothpick always firmly attached to his lips. But father time was passing him by. Bonnie wanted him to "grow up." Get a proper job. Go back to school if he had to. Be clean-cut like Leacy, Robinson, and Garrison. Griffey wouldn't hear of it. He was too proud. He was a big shot.

"Out prowling tonight, are yuh?" one of the guys asked.

"Yeah," Griffey said, chomping on his toothpick. "What's up? Anything cooking?"

"Yeah, Phillips is in town."

"Is he?" Griffey looked up at the guys, as he shut the motor off.

"And he's lookin' for yuh."

"Yeah?"

"That thing of his is sounding like a real bitch."

Griffey played it cool. "That so?" He fell into a silence. Bruce Phillips hailed from Williams, less than an hour west down Route 66. He owned a two-tone, black-and-white 1956 Chevy Nomad Wagon. Word was out he had dropped in one of the new small block 327 engines with some extras. Griffey finally grunted. "It's a small block. He won't touch me."

"He's got two four-barrels. One of the high-lift cams. He bored the cylinders out a few inches, too."

"So what?"

"Just thought we'd tell yuh."

At that moment, the Chevy Nomad Wagon they were referring to flew down the highway. No one spoke again until the red tail lights disappeared around a bend a half-mile away.

"There he goes."

Griffey chomped on his toothpick. "The night's young. I'm ready when he is." He fired up the motor, revving it a few times. He could see customers in Karen's Diner looking over. "See yuh, boys," he said.

* * * *

Griffey found Phillips parked in his Nomad—lights on—on a dark, downtown Flagstaff side street. Griffey parked across from him in the opposite direction and rolled down the window. Both engines were idling. They were only a few feet apart, close enough to talk.

Griffey twirled the toothpick around in his mouth. "What's up, Bruce?" he said to the driver with the blonde brush cut.

"Nothing much. You?"

"Driving around."

"Me, too, I guess."

"Sounds pretty hefty."

"It is."

"I hear you're running two-fours."

"You heard right."

Griffey smirked. "You're gonna need more than two-fours to keep up with me."

"You think so, do yuh?" Phillips replied firmly.

"I know so. See you up on the North Road at the junction. One o'clock."

Phillips lit a cigarette before he answered. He waited, blew out a smoke ring and said, "You can bet on it. Fifty bucks."

"Make it seventy-five."

"Yuh got it. See yuh there."

The North Road was packed with about one hundred spectators by the time Griffey screeched his arrival in his roadster a few minutes before one in the morning. Rick Robinson stood a few feet away, flashlight clenched in his fist. He flicked it on and off twice. As the starter, he was ready.

The two cars lined up side by side in the night on the narrow two-lane road. Robinson flicked the flashlight on and left it on, walking out twenty-five feet ahead and in-between the rumbling cars. He faced the light towards the racers. The revs from both cars increased. The ground was shaking beneath him.

Then he flicked the light out.

Phillips took Griffey from the standing stop, while both cars left a billowing trail of tire smoke at the starting line. But Griffey soon caught up just as the two shifted into second gear so close to each other

116

that they sounded as one. Then Phillips began to pull away. One car length. . . two. . . Griffey could see that he was going to lose. *The money. His reputation. Everything.* In third gear, Phillips was two car lengths in the lead. The finish line—two flashlight blinks—was coming up. Then it happened. In fourth gear, Griffey zoomed ahead by a wide margin. . . passing by the men holding the flashlights, the speedometer reaching over one hundred miles per hour.

It took Griffey nearly another quarter of a mile to slow down and turn around. He idled his hot machine up to the finish line. He got out and looked down the road towards the Phillips Nomad sitting still, lights on.

"What happened?" he asked one of the young men at the line.

"He blew a shift. He's probably picking up all the parts."

Griffey smiled painfully. He was lucky. Phillips had him beat. Beat bad.

Phoenix

When Jimmie Whitman tapped at her porch door, Linda was waiting, thin jacket draped over her arm. She was a perky redhead who wore jeans and a yellow t-shirt with runners. It was only a few minutes after sun-up on Saturday morning. It would hit at least ninety today here in the low valley.

"All set?"

"Sure am," she replied, anxious to go.

They kissed, quick and light on the lips.

Whitman and his girlfriend, Linda Beel, set out for their trip to the Grand Canyon in the Corvette. They had to leave early for the two-hundred-mile trek in order to make it back to Flagstaff by evening. Her mother was emphatic about that. *Stay overnight with Aunt Jill and Uncle George.* They took the scenic route, top down, through Sedona, where the stunning terra cotta cliffs basked in the Arizona sunshine. Then they climbed the winding road, slow and sure into pine country, where it was much cooler. Linda whipped her jacket on. They stopped at the scenic lookout that viewed the heavily-forested valley and Highway 89 below.

They got out of the Corvette, walked hand-in-hand a hundred feet or so, and peered over the rail, inhaling the crisp, dry air at more than a mile above sea level.

Whitman spoke first, smiling. "Beautiful, isn't it."

"I'll say it is."

They pondered each other's eyes.

"Linda?"

"Yes?"

"I was going to do this at the Canyon. But, ah hell, I couldn't wait."

"Do what?"

Whitman dug into his coat for something and held it in his grasp, fist down.

"What's that?" she asked.

He turned his hand upwards and opened his fist. There was a small, red, velvet box. With the other hand, he popped it open.

"Oh, my!" Linda squealed, staring at a sparkling diamond ring.

Whitman got down on one knee. "Linda Beel, will you marry me?"

She glanced around, slightly embarrassed. A few people were smiling at them, noticing what was happening. Blushing, she said, "I don't know what to say," she giggled.

"Say, yes, dammit!" an elderly, black woman uttered. "You'll never get a more romantic proposal than that, sweetie." Others around laughed.

"Do what the lady says," Whitman grinned, glancing over his shoulder at the middle-aged woman standing off to the side.

"Of course, it's yes," Linda said, grinning back, giving in. "Yes! Now stand up so I can kiss you, properly."

An hour later, they reached the plateau, where the university town of Flagstaff sat nestled in clumps of Ponderosa pine. Off to the north were the 10,000-foot-plus San Francisco Peaks. Giddy, they stopped for lunch at a clean roadside hamburger joint, The Gateway, on Sante Fe Avenue, part of Route 66. They ordered burgers with extra cheese, french-fries, and cokes from a window booth.

"Are you sure you want to go through this?" Linda asked, holding Whitman's hand on the table. "I won't finish my nurses training for another two years."

"You still have your part-time job in the department store. Besides, I got a raise last week."

"You did? I didn't know that."

"We'll do just fine."

"Yeah," she nodded, glancing down at the engagement ring on her finger. "You're right. We will."

"Next year?"

"The Spring. June. The month of our birthdays."

"June, it'll be. But we better check with your parents first."

"They won't argue. They like you. I know my dad will probably ask what took you so long."

"Yeah," he chuckled. "We've only been dating on and off for nearly four years."

"But who's counting."

"I've started saving for a house. We can rent for now, though. The first year or so."

"Even after the money you've spent on your car."

"It's not just any car. It's a fuel-injected Corvette."

She looked down the aisle at the waitress bringing their food on a platter.

"Here come the burgers."

Although Linda and Jimmie had been to the canyon before on separate occasions with their families, it was now altogether different as a young couple engaged to be married in a year. Mesmerized, they stood in the early afternoon at Yaki Point, one of the lookouts on the South Rim closest to the park entrance.

"What a sight," Whitman said, holding Linda close. It was on the chilly side this high up, despite the strong sun. It was even higher in elevation than the scenic lookout on Highway 89. The sun brought out brilliant reds, oranges, and yellows in the rock. They saw the Colorado River a mile down below. Through the binoculars Whitman had with him, he could see people—mere dots—near a lodge in the bottom of the valley. Packers, probably.

He scanned across the miles of vivid-colored rock formations. "Maybe I should have proposed to you here, after all."

She kissed him on the neck. "If you did, I might've fallen over the rail."

"In shock?"

"No. . . in excitement."

They laughed, then kissed.

* * * *

119

Later that afternoon they returned to Flagstaff, dropped in on Linda's aunt and uncle for dinner, then sped away to tour the town in the Corvette as the sun was setting to sample a little of the neon nightlife. Whitman saw some hot cars parked by The Gateway and turned into the lot.

Whitman's attention fell on the clean, bone-white 1962 Chevy Impala hardtop. He saw the chrome V-8 insignia on the driver's side fender. Either 283 or a 327, he guessed. Next to it was a dark-purple Thunderbird with a white top. *Not bad.* Then he saw the green '32 roadster off to the right. He chuckled at the painted flames on the fenders as he drove slowly by.

"That's a wild one," Linda said.

Whitman grunted. "Flames are out."

"I think they're cute."

"Pretty tough, though. He's probably got a 409 in that thing."

"It must be a real bitch."

Whitman shot a glance at her. "What did you just say?"

"Isn't that what the car guys say when a car is hot?"

"Yeah, but I didn't think you heard it."

"I wasn't born yesterday, you know."

Whitman smiled and braked at the same time for two young men crossing in front of him. "Hi," he said, as they came over.

"Hi, yourself," one of them said. "We were watching you from the diner."

"Were yuh now," Whitman answered, looking up at the men through the rolled-down window.

"Yeah. Where yuh from?"

"Phoenix."

"Some pretty fast cars down there in the valley, I bet?"

"Yeah. A few. Which cars are yours?"

"Mine's the T-bird," one said.

"I own the Impala," said the other.

"What's the fastest up here in the North country?"

"Griffey's '32. She's the meanest machine on the plateau."

"You don't say?"

Suddenly, Warren Griffey appeared in a black leather jacket, greased-black dark hair, a toothpick between his lips. "You met my friends, I see."

"Yeah."

"Like what you see here?" Griffey said, moving around the driver's side of Whitman's Corvette.

"Yeah, I do," Whitman said. "Yours the '32?"

"You bet."

"409?"

"Yeah."

"Pretty bitchin good for homegrown."

Griffey huffed. "What yuh got under *your* hood?"

"327. Injected."

"Sounds like it. Not bad for factory stuff. Looks brand spanking new."

"It is. Just broke it in. Fifteen hundred miles."

"In that case, let's see what she can do."

"You challenging me?"

"Yeah, my fifty against your fifty."

Linda glanced over at Whitman. "Take it easy," she advised him.

Whitman ignored her and said to Griffey, "What, no odds?"

Griffey chomped on his toothpick. "Odds?"

"Yeah, odds."

"*Jimmie!*" Linda said, louder than before.

He ignored her again. "You're supposed to be the fastest on the plateau. The odds should be at least two-to-one. You're the champ around here. You should be giving odds. Still wanna go for fifty bucks?"

Griffey thought about it, looking around at his friends, Robinson and Garrison. "You're on. Two-to-one odds. Ten o'clock tonight. North Road. Yuh know where that is?"

"No, I don't."

"Off the 180 to the right. Five miles out of here."

"OK. Seeing that you picked the place, I pick the signal man."

"Sounds fair. Who did you have in mind?"

Whitman glanced over at Linda.

Word got around town fast. A good fifty spectators were on hand by ten that evening on the narrow, two-lane road north of town. And no cops. Whitman arrived two minutes after Griffey. They both emerged from their cars at the same time and faced each other.

Robinson began to explain. "This driveway is the starting line. Your girlfriend, here—"

"Linda is my name," Linda said, annoyed. "And I'm his fiancée."

"OK, Linda will walk out fifteen feet in front of you two, face away from you guys, flick the flashlight on, and leave it on. She will face you, count off anywhere from four to six seconds, whatever you prefer, then flick the light out. That's the green light to go, once it's off. OK?"

Griffey and Whitman nodded.

Linda took a breath. "Got it."

"Any questions?"

"Yeah, where's the finish line?" Whitman asked.

"Two flashlights on either side of the road, up ahead. They'll come on as soon as you leave the line."

"Right."

"I hope you know what you're doing, Jimmie," Linda said, softly.

Griffey dug for a clean toothpick in his jeans pocket. "Gonna chicken out, Phoenix boy?"

"Not me, Fastman," Whitman replied. "Let's go. Four seconds?"

"Agreed," Griffey said.

Before Whitman climbed into his Corvette, Robinson patted him on the arm. "Good luck. You're gonna need it."

"We'll see," Whitman replied.

Griffey and Whitman lined their cars up side-by-side on the road, Griffey on the left.

Whitman gripped the floor shifter and revved the fuel-injected engine. The Corvette rocked back and forth with each movement on the gas pedal. He glanced across at Griffey, revving his 409. He looked out at Linda, her back to the racers. She turned around, quickly, flashlight on and facing slightly down. *One. . . two. . . three. . . four. . .* The light went out, and both racers tore a patch of rubber on the road, leaving behind a huge cloud of white-blue smoke from the screeching tires. Whitman had his adversary by half a car length shifting into second gear at 6,000 RPM. By third gear, he was more than two car lengths in the lead.

Fourth gear coming up!

Griffey couldn't believe the Corvette's power. And his own '32 was running up to snuff. Then it happened. He veered too far left, his left-side tires catching the gravel. Trying to steer back to the right, he nudged the wheel too much and the roadster started to swerve. *Left. . . then right.* Then it hit the gravel again. By now, Griffey didn't know what to do at nearly one hundred miles per hour. But it was no use. *The roadster was out of control.*

Whitman could see the trouble from his rear-view mirror, as he crossed the two-flashlight finish line. He saw the roadster swerving, then tumbling into the ditch behind him. He was so engrossed with the sight that it took him longer than normal to hit the brakes and slow down. He turned the Corvette around just as the roadster burst into a red-orange fireball. Whitman poured on the gas and roared by the two people at the finish line. The first one to arrive at the scene, he hit the brakes opposite the ditch where the roadster had landed upside down.

Whitman jumped out of his Corvette. He tried to get closer to the hotrod, but couldn't. The heat from the flames was too intense. He looked around and couldn't see Griffey. Had he gotten out? Then. . . he saw his head leaning on the dash. Spectators began to arrive in cars. Crying, Linda jumped out from the passenger side of Robinson's T-Bird and ran for Whitman. She reached for his arms.

"Oh. . . *Jimmie,* I thought it was you." She kissed him repeatedly on the neck, on the lips, on his cheeks. "Oh, baby, I'm so glad you're all right."

"Slow down, I'm OK," he said, pulling her away. "But he's not."

Robinson ran up to the couple. He stared back at Griffey's roadster. "Oh, God, no."

North of Flagstaff—June, 1973

Jimmie Whitman kept a steady sixty miles per hour on Highway 180 South heading to Flagstaff in his 1972 Plymouth station wagon. Night had fallen. The stars were out in a clear, calm sky. He glanced over at Linda sleeping soundly in the passenger seat. On this, their tenth anniversary, the Whitmans had driven up to the Grand Canyon earlier in the day, the first time in ten years. The two girls were at home for the weekend with Linda's parents.

Linda was a full-time nurse earning good pay. Jimmie owned his own car repair shop and had four employees. They were seven years into a mortgage on a $40,000 bungalow in an affluent neighborhood in Scottsdale, outside Phoenix. Times were good. The couple had put on some weight. They were happy. And they were together, which was more than they could say for so many people they knew who had already gone through one divorce coming out of the free-spirited, free-loving sixties.

Jimmie saw the lights of Flagstaff ahead. He began to slow down. He recognized the spot. *The North Road.* He didn't know why, but he felt he should turn onto it. As he braked, Linda woke.

"Where are we?" she asked, sitting up.

He turned and pressed the gas pedal. "The North Road."

"What are you doing here? Flagstaff's the other way."

"I know."

It took Linda and Jimmie many years to get over that night in 1962 near this same spot. Warren Griffey had died in the mishap. Whitman was never charged. He and the spectators left the scene before the police and the ambulance got there. Jimmie sold the Corvette two years later.

Driving up the road for a couple miles, Jimmie could see two headlights in the rear view mirror coming up behind him awfully quick. In a flash, a car flew by him so fast that all the couple could tell was that it was painted green. Then it raced away into the night over a rise.

"What the hell!" Linda said. "Is that guy crazy? He must be doing a hundred miles an hour."

"At least. Did you hear that roar?" Jimmie added. "That must be some engine."

"Let's get out of here."

"Yeah, let's."

Jimmie drove over the rise to turn around but instead was forced to pile on the brakes. Less than a hundred feet away were two bright headlights, shining right at him. The couple sat stunned, not saying a word. Jimmie pulled onto the shoulder and shut his motor off. They both got out and stood looking at the headlights. The distant car wasn't moving. The motor was idling. High performance, for sure, thought Jimmie.

"What's going on?"

"I don't know," Jimmie replied. "But he's blocking our way."

"Let's just turn around. Flagstaff is the other way, anyway."

The couple got into the wagon, and Jimmie sped away in the other direction.

Jimmie glanced in the rear-view. The headlights were closing in on them. "Here it comes again."

This time the car came up right behind them, stayed back at two car lengths, then pulled out alongside. It stayed there for a second or two, then drove off. All they could see now were narrowing tail lights.

Jimmie swallowed hard. "Did you see that? Just like that green roadster with the suicide doors."

"Yeah. It even had the flames on the side."

An eerie feeling came over the couple. Jimmie stopped the wagon on the shoulder and shut the engine off. He stepped onto the pavement.

"What are you doing?" Linda asked, stepping out with him.

"Listen."

They heard the flat-out motor roar in the clear night.

"What?"

"That's a 409. Nobody runs 409s anymore. Chevy hasn't made that engine in years. This is spooky.

"It sure is."

"Let's get out of here."

In town, the Whitmans entered The Gateway on Route 66. Times had changed. No longer a hamburger joint with hot cars out front, The Gateway was now a family restaurant that served liquor.

"So, it's still here," Jimmie commented, glancing around. "It looks better than I last remember. You hungry?"

"After what happened out there, I could use a stiff one, instead."

"You mean a drink?"

Linda frowned. "Yeah!"

"I'll join yuh."

They slid into a booth near the kitchen. They saw the place was only a quarter full, well past the prime dinner hour. Two girls in a booth near them were wearing the latest fashion. Hot pants. Through the glass, Jimmie saw a movie theater. "Want to see a movie after? *The Poseidon Adventure* is playing."

Linda glanced over her shoulder at the bright red and white neon sign. "At least it's not *Deep Throat*."

Jimmie laughed.

A chubby waiter in his mid-twenties appeared, brandishing a pen and a paper pad.

"What can I do for you, folks?"

"Can I ask you a question before I order?"

"Sure, I guess."

"We're from Phoenix. Are there no hot cars around Flagstaff anymore?"

The waiter chuckled. "Not for a long time. Back in the fifties and early sixties, there were a lot of them. No more. Not since the cops cracked down in. . . oh. . . 1962 or was it 1963. A hotrod burnt up on the North Road, driver died. After that, cops were everywhere. They didn't allow anything. No side pipes. No cheater slicks. No noisy mufflers. And no street racing."

"Well, fellah, I saw a real hot one. A green roadster on the North Road. Looked like she was right out of the past. It flew by us at over a hundred miles an hour. Nearly blew us off the road, the crazy son of a gun."

The man looked at the other customers. "A green roadster you say?" he said, softly.

"Yeah. A Ford. A '32. Suicide doors. Flames on the side. I heard the motor. It had to be a 409. No 396 or 427 sounds like that."

"Wait right here," the man whispered, then hurried off to the kitchen.

"What was that all about?"

Jimmie shrugged at his wife. "Search me."

Another man returned. He was the couple's age and he had an apron on.

"You look familiar," Jimmie said. Then it came to him. His hair had receded, but it was still him. "I remember you. You had the '55 T-Bird."

The man tried to smile. "Rick Robinson. I own this place now. So, you came back."

"Yeah, we did."

Then he leaned over the table, and lowered his voice. "I heard you saw a roadster on the North Road."

"Yeah, looked just like the machine I raced back in 1962. It even sounded like a 409."

"It *was* a 409." Robinson wiped his forehead. "Look, can I sit down?"

"Sure." Jimmie moved over.

"Listen. You're about the fifth person in the last year or so who's seen something on that stretch. People are saying it's haunted, you know."

"Haunted?"

"Yeah. By you-know-who."

"That fellah I raced?"

"Yeah. Warren Griffey."

126

"Come on!"

"Really. Every so often on a clear night, you can drive out of town and stop your car. You can hear Griffey's machine. I know. I've heard it. Others have seen the lights, too. Some have even seen the '32 Ford come right up alongside them."

"That happened to us," Jimmie said.

"What are you saying?" Linda asked. "It's a ghost?"

"Call it whatever you want. Ghost. Phenomenon. I knew Griffey. His engine with that 4-barrel carb had a sound all its own. Unmistakable." He sighed. "Look, I'd better get back in the kitchen."

"Sure," Jimmie said.

Robinson spun around. "By the way. Order what you want. It's on the house. For old time's sake. I'll send Billy back."

The couple stared at each other.

"Geez," Jimmie sighed. "What do you know?"

10

Going Broke

America was changing in the mid-sixties. In every way. Kennedy was gunned down, turning federal politics upside-down. Vietnam was heating up, ready to explode. Civil Rights were an issue. In music, the good, ol' rock-n-roll of Elvis and Chuck Berry gave way to the British invasion and long hair. The big and fast Interstates were heading West, hitting the more-populated East first. A piece at a time. State by state. Thousands of businesses along Route 66 were facing financial ruin with the coming of the super highways, forcing some people to take drastic action.

SOUTH-CENTRAL MISSOURI—FEBRUARY, 1964

Motel owner Michael Cook squinted through the venetian blinds of his lobby window. Only a few rooms were occupied this cold, cloudy afternoon. Then again, it was the middle of winter with two inches of snow on the ground. Profits would pick up in the spring and summer. It always did ever since 1948, the year he and his wife had this attractive place built on the highway in the middle of Missouri, half-way between St. Louis and the Kansas border. The couple had conducted a thriving operation for years, counting on the traffic of Route 66 only a hundred feet away. Customers loved the place, so peaceful and serene in the Ozark Mountains, surrounded by cottonwoods, cedars, and pines at the base of the steep cliff called Penner's Peak. The rooms were clean. The service was friendly. Air-conditioning in the summer. It was a gold mine.

Then he heard about the interstate.

With the opening of I-44, all that would soon change. His busi-ness—The Emerald Springs Motor Court—would dry up completely, twenty miles off the nearest section of the new four-lane monster slated to be completed sometime in late autumn or early winter. Construction had already started in parts of Missouri. I-44 was coming, despite many business people along Route 66 who had tried to stop it. It was no use. It was only a matter of time. No one would take a twenty-mile detour off I-44 to stop off in the middle of nowhere for the night. Route 66 through these parts would only be a memory. His place was too small. The big hotels would soon pop up along I-44 and take over, pushing out the little guy. That was the trouble with this country now—inter-states, big companies, and rock-n-roll. He grunted, thinking of the Ed Sullivan Show last night on TV. Those shaggy Beatles with their *yeah, yeah, yeah* songs. *Bunch of long-haired, commie pinkos from England.*

Cook lit a cigarette, contemplating his predicament, moping around, watching the traffic on Route 66. It was busy today. About another year of this, then that's it. No more gravy train. At fifty-two years old, gray-haired and paunchy, he knew he didn't stand a snowball's chance in hell at starting another business or getting another job. What could he do? Sell? Who'd buy the place, this far off the interstate.

He had a year to make a decision. A miracle would be more like it. Out the window, his eyes fell on a half-ton truck rolling off Route 66 and onto the circular, gravel driveway in front of the office. The driver, dressed in blue coveralls, got out. It was his friend, Jack Creighton, who managed the gas-and-repair station a mile down the road.

Creighton opened the lobby door. "Hey, Mike. How yuh doing?"

"Could be better, I guess."

"I fixed your Caddy. Plugged fuel line, that's all. Running like a charm. I'll give her the tune-up you asked for then bring her around about three. Won't be much. Forty bucks, at the most."

"Fine. Thanks."

"I figured that would be good news. You OK? You look down about something."

"Ah, just thinking about what I'll do by the end of the year."

Creighton heaved a sigh. "Tough one, ain't it."

"Yeah. What about you?"

"No alternative but to close shop."

"Really?"

"Yeah. Hell, it's paid for. I'll take my early retirement. Fifty-eight is close enough. I'll let the two young boys go and board the place up."

Cook shrugged his shoulders. "I still got the renovation bills from four years back. And I don't have enough money saved. You know, what I can't figure out is why the Interstate has to take such a wide bend in these parts. Every other place through Missouri and Illinois it's been within five or six miles at the most from Route 66. What the hell gives?"

"The rock around here, I guess. Not to mention the wildlife reserve down the road. The I-44 will cut right through it. Anyway, I dropped by to tell you I may have found a solution for yuh." Creighton grinned.

"Yeah, what?"

"I know some people."

"Who?"

"Can we talk somewhere, in private?"

"Sure. Come on out back to the den. Should I get my wife?"

"No, I don't think that's a good idea. Just you."

Cook thought that odd. "Oh... OK. Want a beer?"

"Yeah, that'll hit the spot."

With fresh snow falling that night, Cook drove his white Cadillac to the lookout point five miles west off Route 66 and parked beside a Chevy sedan on the gravel. He found the footpath to the left through the pine and rocks in the dark and was ready to follow it, when two figures jumped out at him.

"Cook?"

There stood two men in black coats, hats on, faces unseen.

"You got him."

"Got the cash?" The voice sounded young. Someone in his twenties or early thirties.

"Yeah."

"Two thousand now and another two thousand when the job is done. Right?"

"That was the deal." Cook handed a white envelope to one of the men who snatched it off him.

"When will you do it?"

"Tomorrow."

"That soon?"

"Yeah. We can't wait around, you know."

"All right, then. The best time is morning, after the eleven o'clock checkout. Around eleven-thirty. My wife will be gone into town on an appointment. You're going to make it look like an accident, aren't you?"

"Sure, we will. A cigarette that someone didn't douse. And remember, you'll be in the house away from the scene, so you don't recognize us when we make our getaway."

"I remember. Fair enough."

"We'll be in and out before you know it. Just make sure the rooms are cleared out."

"I will. By the way, how many of these have you done?"

"Lots."

"Just do it right. I don't want to be pinned with this thing."

"Don't you worry, old man. We'll take care of everything."

"You'd better."

"See you back here in two nights. Same time. Don't forget to bring the rest of the money with yuh."

"Do it right and I will," Cook said, swaggering off.

All the customers were gone by fifteen minutes after eleven and Cook made his rounds to be sure the whole place was vacated. His wife had left for the nearby town of Rolla shortly after ten. She wouldn't be back until well after twelve, she figured. *Perfect.* He walked to the house, leaving fresh footprints in the overnight snow that had stopped falling by three that morning. He threw off his coat and shoes and stood by the kitchen window, puffing on a cigarette.

All he could do was hurry up and wait.

Exactly at eleven-thirty, the Chevy sedan from the night before steered into the driveway and was soon blocked out of Cook's view by the motor court office. Cook turned away and switched the radio on. He didn't want to look.

Inside the Emerald office, the two scruffy men, Bud, the leader, and Donnie, went about their dirty deed by pouring cans of paint thinner on the furniture and pine floor in the lobby and onto the carpets in the two halls to the left and the right that connected the entire complex

132

of rooms. Then they took the empty cans to the car and threw them in the trunk.

"Here goes nothing," Bud announced, standing in the left hallway, holding a lit cigarette. He walked towards the entrance door, Donnie following. Then Bud dropped the butt on the pine floor. The entrance quickly burst into a lick of flames.

"Shit, someone's coming!" Donnie yelled, pointing to the driveway.

They gawked out the lobby window. It was a white Cadillac. The wife had come back early. "Damn it! The bitch is here."

"Here she comes in the front. Let's scram!" Donnie screamed.

"Come on! We can't use the front now! Out the side!"

They ran down the left hall, closest to their car, the flames following them. They flew out the door and around the corner, just as Fae Cook stood outside the front door in shock.

Her attention shot from the burning lobby to the two men. . . back to the lobby. "Hey!" she shouted, finding her tongue. "Stop, you two! STOP!"

Donnie and Bud jumped into the Chevy and drove off, spraying Cook's wife with snow and gravel as she tried to chase after them.

She stopped. "FIRE!" she yelled to no apparent person. "FIRE!"

By the time the Rolla Fire Department got to the scene, the Emerald Motor Court was too far damaged to save anything. The only thing left to do was put the fire out.

The next day, the fire chief and his young assistant kicked through the blackened remains of the lobby. The chief glanced around and sniffed. "Smell that?"

"What?"

"You don't smell it?"

The assistant shook his head. "Nothing in particular."

"I got a nose for this stuff."

The chief had been a fireman for thirty years. He also had a very sensitive nose. Some called it the best in the business. And it always seemed to detect something the first time in a fire-damaged place. "I want some samples collected, throughout the whole place."

"Yes, sir."

"Then I want them sent to the lab in St. Louis. Right away. Put a rush on it."

"You bet."

"Good man." The chief winked at his assistant. "Stick with me and you might learn something."

The assistant grinned. "I hope I will."

In the house, a tall, uniformed policeman sat at the kitchen table questioning the middle-aged couple.

"OK, you say you never saw the two guys before?" He opened a small notepad and began to jot some notes with a ball-point pen.

Cook exhaled cigarette smoke. "All I saw was the car driving off."

"Did *you* get a good look at them, ma'am?"

"I can't say for sure," Fae said, through tears that made her dark mascara run. "They were kind of dirty. You know, unshaven. They wore baseball caps and black leather jackets. I might be able to identify one of them."

"And you had just pulled up in the driveway when you saw the two men run out of the side?"

"That's right," Fae answered, wiping the tears on a tissue. "For some strange reason, they seemed surprised that I was there."

The policeman's eyebrows moved suspiciously. He continued to write on the pad. "Where were you at the time, Mr. Cook?"

"In the house," Cook answered calmly, holding his wife's hand.

"You say you saw the car drive off?"

"Yes, I did."

"What was the make?"

"Chevy sedan. 1959 or '60. Don't know for sure."

"Color?"

"Brown," Fae recalled. "It had a couple dents in 'er, too."

"Could you make out the model?"

"Nah," Cook said. "I don't know my cars too well."

"Did either of you catch the license plate?"

They both shook their heads.

"I can't remember the numbers, or anything, but they were Missouri plates," she said.

The policeman continued writing. "What were you doing at the time, Mr. Cook?"

"Just about to fix myself a sandwich."

"And you left the motor court unoccupied?"

"That's right."

"Why?"

"I often come back to the house once the customers check out. Then I go back after lunch to clean up, and get the rooms ready for the afternoon customers."

"According to the bank in town, you took out a second mortgage for some renovations to the court four years ago. And you still owe on it. That right?"

"Yeah, that's right," Cook sighed, shifting in his chair. "What does that have to do with anything?"

"Oh, just asking, that's all. Routine. Part of the investigation." The policeman stood. "Oh, by the way, ma'am, sir, why do you suppose someone would want to torch your place?"

"How should I know? Isn't that for you to find out?" Cook snapped. "Just some dumb jerks out for some kicks."

Yeah, *kicks on Route 66* the policeman wanted to say, but held back. He noticed Cook's hand shaking as he drew on his cigarette. "Yeah, I suppose so. I best be going. I'll be in touch."

"I hope you can catch those guys," Fae said.

The policeman tried to smile. "We'll do our best, ma'am."

In the driveway, the policeman and the fire chief conferred by the police car.

"He doesn't look that shook up by it. His wife does, though. What do you make of it?" the policeman asked, although he sensed the answer.

The fire chief chuckled. "Arson. That's for hell sure. I'll have some samples checked out. Either solvent or paint thinner was used. And lots of it. These guys were amateurs. And bad ones at that. They left a trail a mile long."

"No cans around?"

"Nope. They must've gotten rid of them. With the I-44 coming through soon, you think this is another case of a Route 66 businessman collecting on the insurance and moving on?"

The policeman nodded firmly. "Bull's eye. All we have to do is prove it. It don't take a genius to spot a wolf in a chicken coop. Geez, this is an epidemic."

"The only way to nab Cook is to find the arsonists."

"Yeah," the policeman agreed. "That may be tough. I know how these arsonists work. If it's like the other cases, usually no visual contact is made between the owners and the arsonists. It's one thing the arsonists insist on, for their own safety. There's usually a go-between. Anyway, I'm going to poke around. I'll start with that filling station down the road. They may know something."

"Good luck."

"Thanks." The policeman began to walk away.

"I'll let Henry know once the tests come through."

"Do that," the policeman said over his shoulder.

"Jack Creighton?"

Creighton was hunched over the fender of a Ford station wagon in the car bay removing a fuel pump when he heard his name. "That's me," he answered, without looking up. "Hang on a sec, be right with yuh." He turned around, the pump in his greasy hands. The sight of the policeman jarred him at first, but he did his best to recover. "What can I do for you, officer?"

"Can I ask you a few questions?"

"Sure. You must be new. So, where's Henry?"

"He asked me to come out for him."

"Anyway, what's up? Oh, excuse me, I'd better put this down before it leaks all over the blasted place." He took a few steps to a bench. "There," Creighton said.

"You heard about the fire at the Emerald Motor Court?"

"Yeah," Creighton replied, shaking his head. "What a shame."

"Isn't it."

"The Cooks claim they saw a dented, brown 1959 or 1960 Chevy sedan with Missouri plates leaving the property just after the Court burst into flame."

"Is that so?"

"You don't remember a car like that coming or going along here?"

Creighton frowned. "This is Route 66. Cars come and go all along here all the time. I don't have time to stop to notice each individual car that goes by."

"No, you don't, I reckon. But I just thought I'd ask. Besides, they could've filled up here before noon. There's no other gas stations for at least another ten miles or so."

"*Fifteen* miles," Creighton corrected the officer. "And no, they didn't fill up here."

"You're positive about it?"

"Yeah, I am."

"OK, thanks."

In the evening, Cook left his wife in her full-length nightgown trying to laugh at the Beverly Hillbillies on TV, while he made his trek to the lookout point. As he turned into the lot, his headlights shone on a different car, this one a 1961 Plymouth. *They probably stole it,* Cook mused. *Just like they probably stole the other one, too.* He parked the Cadillac in the same spot as last time, and shut the motor and lights off. It was pitch dark. All the snow had melted that day from a mild thaw that had whisked through the Ozarks in the last twenty-four hours.

Cook emerged from the car slowly to find the two men directly in front of them.

"Got the dough?" the one nearest him said.

Cook hesitated. "Part of it."

The man grabbed Cook by the lapel of his coat. "What do you mean, part of it?"

"You only deserve another five hundred."

"Five hundred! Don't monkey around, wise guy. That wasn't the deal. Two thousand down and two thousand when we did the job."

The other man moved in closer.

"You botched it. My wife saw you running out."

"Did she identify us?"

Cook hesitated again. "No, thank God for you."

"You better give us the money, pal, or I'll rip your tongue out through your ears."

"Five hundred is all you get."

"We'll see about that."

"Let me give you some damn good advice. Get away from here, as far from here as you can."

Cook turned for his car, but didn't get there. One of the men grabbed him, twirled him around, and the other man slugged him in the face, knocking Cook to the ground. Together, the men propped him up against the Cadillac, punching him and kicking him repeatedly, until he fell to the ground once more.

"Assholes!" Cook gasped, leaning on one elbow, wiping the blood from his mouth. "You'll never get anything now."

One of the men kicked Cook in the ribs and the head. This time he didn't move or say anything.

Down the road, less than a quarter-mile away, headlights were coming towards them.

"Come on, let's beat it," one of the men said, nervously. "Someone's coming this way."

"Shit! There's always somebody coming!" said the other.

The arsonists drove off in a hurry, spinning gravel at Cook.

Cook waited several moments for his head to clear before he tried to get up, and finally did with great difficulty. He drove home grunting and groaning for the full five miles. On one curve, he nearly drove off the road, but managed to stay on until he steered into the driveway opposite the burned out motor court. Cook shook his head and rested it on the steering wheel. *Everything was going from bad to worse. Why did he listen to Jack?*

He looked up at the house. All the lights were out except for the one in the porch. Fae had gone to bed early. Good. All the better for him to fix himself up as best he could, then crawl into bed without her noticing anything.

Fae Cook drove to the Rolla police station for nine in the morning and met with the policeman who had been to the house. There in a hall, she saw an old friend, Henry Hewitt, a seasoned, fiftyish policeman who had been on the job for over twenty-five years, a person she knew to be honest, straightforward, and impartial in every way.

"Hi there, Fae." Henry was a chubby policeman who had lost nearly all his hair on top. "Too bad we have to meet under such circumstances."

Fae attempted a smile. "It's good to see you, Henry."

"You met young Tom yesterday, I hear."

"Yes, we did. He asked me to drop by. I'd like to help, if I can."

"Good. Shall we get started. I'll get you a cup of coffee. Black with a little sugar, right?"

138

"You remembered. Thanks, I could use a good strong one."

Henry poured her a freshly-made batch from the counter in the next room, then the three of them hung a right into another room two doors down and all sat at a chipped oak table. Tom had two large, thick books under one arm and was ready to open the first one.

"I should tell you something first, though," Fae said, taking the first mouthful of coffee.

"What?" Henry answered.

"When I left my husband this morning, he was still sleeping. I noticed. . ."

"Go on. Noticed what?"

She winced. "He had bruises all over his face something awful."

Henry glanced over at Tom. The two didn't seem that surprised.

"When did he get them?"

She shrugged. "Last night some time, I suppose. He went out. Said he was going into town. He was fine then. I went to bed early. I woke up this morning and there he was, all swollen. Do you think it has anything to do with all this?"

Henry and Tom exchanged glances, nodding.

"Maybe it does," Henry replied. "For now, why don't you get on with the book."

Tom opened to the first page of photographs. "We have here two books of black-and-white snapshots. All are men who have records in the state of Missouri. Big and small. Petty thievery. What have you. Look through them carefully. Take your time."

"If it takes you all day, that's just fine, too," Henry added. "I'll order out for some sandwiches by noon. I'm just going to step out on some other business. Tom will look after you. OK?"

"Sure. Thanks, Henry."

Henry walked the length of the hall and was stopped by another policeman. "Call for you, sir. Your line."

"Thanks."

"By the way, sir. A '59 Chevy was reported stolen. And it fits the description. We got a call this morning."

"Figures."

Henry turned the corner and picked up the receiver in his office. "Sergeant Hewitt, here."

"Henry, it's Bill," the caller said. "We got the tests back. It was paint thinner, all right. In the halls. In the lobby. Everywhere."

"So, we got him by the short hairs."

"What's next?"

"Find our arsonists. We may know something soon, I hope."

"Anything else you want?"

"Nothing right now. Thanks, Bill."

"Keep me posted."

"Sure." Henry clicked the receiver in place. "Mike Cook," he said to himself. "What's this world coming to?"

By ten-thirty, and two cups of coffee later, Fae was nearly finished with the first book. She looked over at Tom who was trying to stay awake in his chair against the wall. She turned to the last three pages. Then... in the middle of the second-last page was a snapshot of a man in his twenties. *Square jaw. Hook nose. Bushy eyebrows. Unshaven face.* She sighed. She glanced up at the ceiling then back to the photo. She closed her eyes for a moment to think back to the two men running from their motor court. Then she opened them. It was *him* without the cap. He was the one who got behind the wheel of the dented Chevy sedan.

Tom looked over at her. "Mrs. Cook, do you see someone?"

"Yes, I think I do."

He jerked from his chair, and came over. "Are you sure?"

"Yes," she nodded, pointing to the picture. "He was the driver. It's him."

"Hold that thought. I'll be right back."

Tom returned with Henry in seconds.

Henry stared at the photo and the name underneath. "Bud Peele." He grinned. "Fae, are you absolutely sure that's one of the men you saw running out of your place?"

"Positive."

"Bud Peele, eh? We finally got the bastard. Oh, sorry, Fae."

"That's OK. He is a bastard."

"Who *is* he?" Tom asked.

"A two-bit thug. A car thief," Henry replied. "I sent him up once, myself. So he's into torching buildings now. And he has an accomplice. Tom, go send out a state-wide bulletin. You'll find all the details on him in the file."

"Yes, sir." The policeman trotted off.

Henry faced his old friend. "Thanks loads for coming by, Fae."

"You're welcome."

"Thanks to you, we got our man. One of them anyway. But he'll lead us to the other."

One day later, on a bright, sunny afternoon, Henry dropped by the motor court with Tom and another policeman who drove a second car. The three officers assembled at the bottom of the steps to the house.

"Listen you guys. It's only Mike we want. I'm sure Fae didn't have anything to do with it, not with how she identified Peele for us."

Henry shook his head. He still couldn't believe it. Mike Cook, a man Henry admired for years. They had visited each other. Ate at each other's houses. Their kids were friends.

"A shame," Tom said, speaking of the motor court. "It was a nice place."

"I know." Henry sighed. "Let's get this over with."

Henry ambled up the steps, the two others behind him, and rapped at the wooden door. Cook answered in a grubby t-shirt. *Yeah, he has bruises,* Henry noted.

"Afternoon, Mike."

"Hi, Henry. Come on in."

"I'd rather stay right here. We caught the men who torched your place, Mike. And their other accomplice, Jack Creighton. All three admitted to conspiring to burn down your motor court, so that you could collect the insurance. And they implicated you. Geez, Mike. I hate to do this. But, you're under arrest. You have the right to—"

"Forget it. I'll go." Cook swallowed, looking back to his wife at the kitchen table. He sighed, bit his bottom lip, and faced the policemen. "I knew you'd be coming for me sooner or later."

"We suspected you right from the beginning."

"I don't doubt it."

"You're not the first one along Route 66 to try such a thing."

Fae heard the conversation and stood. Enraged, she walked over and slapped her husband on the side of the head.

He pushed her away. "What did you do that for?"

"How could you!" She wound up to slap him again, but Henry and Tom stepped between the couple.

"I did it for us! For you!"

"Thanks a lot!" she screamed, as they took her husband away. "At least we had something before. Now we have nothing, and you're going to jail!"

At the station, Cook was placed in a cell. Exhausted, he sat on the cot and began to cry. Two hours later, Fae arrived at the station with a newspaper under her arm.

"Let me see my husband," she demanded.

Henry met her in the hall. "Sure. Come with me."

Fae marched down the hall, to the back, and stood at the metal bars to her husband's cell, slapping the newspaper against the lock. "You idiot! Sometimes, I could. . . just. . . oh! Look at this, you big dope!" She threw the newspaper between the bars. "Look at it. Front page of the *Rolla Chronicle*. The I-44 won't be missing us after all."

"They won't."

"No! It'll be taking a detour and end up less than a mile from the court. They're going to build a ramp only a mile away. We could have kept going. All we needed was a billboard."

Cook picked the paper off the floor to see for himself. His wife was right. The article stated the I-44 had a change to it. A big change. A map showed the entire state of Missouri, where Route 66 was and where the new I-44 would be going. Both routes hugged close right through most of the state. *They did change it.* The closest was a line that ran right up to Penner's Point. . . where the Emerald Motor Court was situated.

Cook slumped onto the cot. "You sore at me, Fae?"

"What do you think?"

"I did it for us. Can't you understand that?"

"Famous last words. Don't expect me to be waiting," Fae said.

11

One Giant Step

By the last year of the sixties, America appeared to be breaking up. Hippies. Free love. Draft-dodging. Pot-smoking. Riots. The war in Vietnam was dividing the nation. The Russians were miles ahead of the Americans in space technology. They had sent the first satellite into orbit around the earth. . . the first man in orbit. . . the first man on a space-walk. . . NASA, the American space program, on the other hand, was floundering. According to President Kennedy in his famous 1961 speech, the Americans would have to pull out all the stops to put a man on the moon before the decade was out. And it had to be done, no matter what.

LOS ANGELES, CALIFORNIA—JULY 19, 1969

The radio personality removed the receiver in his tastefully furnished office at WBID Radio.

"Yeah, Blake Turner here." He heard something on the other end, perhaps a door close. "Hello!" he barked. "Anybody there?"

"Mr. Turner, I need to talk to you."

"So, talk."

"In person."

"Who is this? What's it about?"

"I can't say over the phone."

"Why not? Where are you calling from?"

"Needles. Can you meet me here?"

"*Needles!* Why can't you come to LA?"

"I can't. Can you meet me here, tomorrow?"

"*Apollo 11* is landing on the moon tomorrow."

"I know. At 12:52 to be exact. Eastern."

"How in blazes would you know that?"

"I know a helluva lot about the whole space program. A few things your listeners would love to hear, pal. I got a story that will knock your dirty little shorts off. It'll beat anything you've ever done before. Bigger than the JFK assassination. Be at the Red Lion by ten in the morning. It's right on Route 66, the main drag through Needles. The west side of town. Can't miss it. See yuh."

"Hey, wait. How will I know you?"

"I'll find you."

The person hung up.

Turner huffed. *Needles*, he thought, *it's hotter than a furnace out there in July.* Turner sat down at his desk. It didn't sound like a prank call. It was tempting. *The space program?* He relished anything controversial that he could use on his talk show program that aired nine o'clock every evening on WBID.

But what could be controversial about the first lunar landing in history?

Blake Turner was a living legend in the Los Angeles area. A television personality for years, he switched to radio for more money. He now had one of the most popular programs in that part of the country and it aired on an extremely strong WBID signal that fanned out several hundred miles, drawing in the states of Nevada, Arizona, Oregon, and Utah and well into Mexico. He had contacts, it seemed, everywhere, which often baffled and bothered the censors, the military, the police, and other authorities. He did not support the Vietnam War and told his listeners so. Once, he went so far as to interview two draft dodgers living in Canada. He also wanted to see the legalization of pot, prostitution and abortion.

He agreed with the growing number of discontent Americans who suspected that Lee Harvey Oswald had nothing to do with the JFK assassination. The federal government was behind it, he stated, which was exactly what New Orleans attorney Jim Garrison thought when he arrested Clay Shaw in 1967 and brought him to trial earlier in 1969.

Turner had Garrison on his program two days after the jury let Shaw go. Certain individuals had tried for more than a year to take Turner off the air. WBID wouldn't hear of it, not when their ratings were going through the roof. A major part of the public loved this good-looking, blonde, well-dressed bachelor of forty, who had been causing a stir on the airwaves for the last three years with his show. Even the ones who hated Turner still enjoyed listening to him. He was tough. He was ornery. And he was a jerk. But he was a controversial, interesting jerk.

Needles, California

Norman Norris left the phone booth and made the forty-foot walk to his room as quickly as he could. He was paranoid by now that someone would see him. Not to mention that the thermometer had to be over one-hundred degrees out here at the eastern edge of the Mojave Desert. He could barely breathe. Desert air often bothered his asthma and today was no exception.

He opened the door and welcomed the abrupt temperature change, compliments of the air-conditioner blasting a grinding beat in the window of the second-story motel room. He slid back the curtain of the other window to look down at the Palm Trees on the boulevard and the Red Lion directly across the street.

Just a few more hours.

Blake Turner arrived at the boulevard opposite the Red Lion at ten-to-ten in the morning. Hardly a car or person anywhere. Probably all watching the moon landing. Then again, it was too hot anyway. He didn't step from the air-conditioned Chevy Camaro right off. He left the motor and air running while he listened to the live radio broadcast on WBID of the first-ever moon landing. He loosened his tie and rolled up the sleeves of his white dress shirt, intent on every word. *Apollo 11* which was now only minutes away from touchdown. While the command ship, *Columbia,* orbited the moon, Buzz Aldrin and Neil Armstrong, were setting down to the surface inside the landing module, *Eagle.* Almost there. Everything was on course.

Here it comes, Turner thought. He didn't see the man in sunglasses, beige walking shorts and white t-shirt tap loudly on the window.

Turner jumped, startled. "What the—" He rolled the window down.

"I'm the one who called you yesterday. Let's go inside." He listened. "Never mind the radio. We can watch it on TV."

Inside the Red Lion, Norris and Turner sat in the back corner of the packed lounge, the other customers glued to the black-and-white television, watching the live broadcast of the lunar landing. No one was making a sound. The waitresses weren't serving, too engrossed with what they were witnessing.

"So, what's this all about?" Turner asked Norris, who now had his sunglasses off.

"Keep your voice down. Wait until the big show is over."

"Why in the corner? We're too far from the TV."

"I want my back to the wall."

"OK, mister."

"I suppose you want a name? Call me. . . Buzz."

Turner grinned.

"Like Buzz Aldrin?"

"Yeah. Wherever he really is."

Turner stared at the man in an odd way. "Huh?"

"Quiet. We'll talk later. Back in my motel room."

The television screen displayed a fuzzy camera view from the bottom of the lunar module as it moved slowly over the moon's surface. . . closer and closer to touchdown. A crater passed by. They were real close now. They could see the moon dust blurring the image. Then it stopped. A voice came on, confident and calm. "THE EAGLE HAS LANDED."

A thunderous cheer broke the silence. America had landed on the moon!

Norris pointed at his watch. "What did I tell yuh. Twelve-fifty-two."

One of the waitresses came by. "Hi, there."

"Hi," Turner answered.

"What'll it be?"

"Two drafts."

They drank their beers, while they watched Neil Armstrong descend the module ladder. Stepping onto the surface of the moon, he said, with conviction, "THAT'S ONE SMALL STEP FOR MAN. ONE GIANT LEAP FOR MANKIND."

Norris grunted. He turned to Turner and said, "I've seen enough of this shit. Let's go."

Norris unlocked his hotel room and let Turner enter first.

"So, what the hell's the story, pal?"

"None of that crap is true," Norris replied, shutting the door quickly, peering around the window curtain at the street.

Turner gawked at the man. "What?"

"It's all a fake. Sit down and listen to me real good."

And listen Turner did. A technician by trade who had worked for MGM for six years, Norris had come from a secret government installation north of Las Vegas, Nevada, called Area 51. Operated by the CIA. Guarded around the clock. It had been built in the mid-50s for testing the U-2 spy plane. There, Norris had seen many strange things in the last three years. Secret aircraft tested. This was no big news to Turner. He had heard of Area 51 before. But the strangest tale of all was Norris's version of a particular sound stage that was constructed to resemble the moon, complete with black sky. . . sand. . . and mountains in the background. Bright lights were situated to one side to simulate the only light source that can be seen on the moon. . . the sun. While Turner sat in a chair, Norris stood over him and went on to say that two years ago—shortly after the space program's number one pilot, Gus Grissom, had been killed in what the public believed was an accident—his superiors informed him that America had discovered that it was far too dangerous and too costly to really land on the moon. Instead, with the help of trick photography and Hollywood, they would fake it. Grissom didn't go along with it. So, they got rid of him.

Turner let out a whistle. "Why fake it?"

"Come on, Turner. You've been in the business for a few years. To save face, of course," Norris answered. "Think about it. Get people's minds off Vietnam, the Cold War, not to mention the Russians beating us to everything in space. First satellite, first woman in space, first man, first animal. They beat us at everything. The United States has to come out smelling like a rose. And they will. Because they have the technology to fake it. The Russians don't. They don't have the special effects of Hollywood."

"Why will it be dangerous to go to the moon?"

"Too much radiation out beyond the earth. Ever hear of the Van Allen Radiation Belts?"

"Yeah, I guess."

"They're a thousand miles away. NASA never could figure out how to get through them without frying the spacecraft and the men inside. Another thing, it's almost 300 degrees on the sun side of the moon's surface. Those skimpy little spacesuits won't stop the heat or the sun's radiation. Not a chance."

Turner jumped to his feet. "You're supposed to be back at Area 51, aren't you?"

"Right on. I left and never went back. I just couldn't take it anymore. They're probably looking for me right now."

"Where are you going to go?"

"Mexico is probably my only choice."

"How?"

"I came here with my own car. But I'll have to leave it. I'll have to get another one. I'll try a rental, then walk away from it once I'm over the border."

"Take the back roads there. I'm sure whoever is looking for you will be checking the main highways."

"I figured that."

"There's one thing bothering me, Buzz."

"What's that?"

"How do I know you're telling the truth? Where's the proof?"

Norris got on his knees and dug under the bed. He opened a suitcase and pulled out a large manila envelope. "Here," he said, handing the envelope to Turner. "Copies I made in the lab. Photographs of men on the moon. Already taken ahead of time, by yours truly. The ones they will probably use for magazines and newspapers. *Time Magazine*, for sure."

Norris reached over and grabbed one of the photos, a bright, color photo of a man in a white space suit, images reflecting off the glass of his helmet.

It sure looked like the moon, Turner thought. Barren ground. Black background. Bright light source. He studied all three photos for several seconds. They did look real!

Norris snatched the photos back, threw them in the envelope, and returned them to the suitcase. "Well? Do you think I'm crazy. . . or what?" He kicked the suitcase under the bed.

"I don't know. . ."

Norris smiled. "Don't tell me the great Blake Turner is tongue-tied."

"I am. I have to admit, I am."

"Blows your mind, doesn't it."

"To put it bluntly, yeah. *Hell, yeah.* So," Turner eyed Norris suspiciously, "what do you want?"

"Nothing."

"You're kidding."

"Expose it. That's all. Just give me a chance to get the hell out of the country first."

"You don't want any money?"

"Nope. Not a cent."

"That's a switch. Hey, wait a minute." Turner snapped his fingers. "I've got a great idea."

"And that is?"

"Call me from Mexico. Right on the program. You can expose this hoax all over the radio airwaves. You don't even have to give your name."

"I don't plan to."

"What do you say?"

"I never thought of that. But, yeah, that could work."

"It's the only way to do it. The whole program will be about you and what you're willing to tell."

"OK, Turner. I'll do it. One giant step for man. *One giant hoax for mankind.*"

Turner nodded, smiling. "I like that. Can I use it on the show?"

"Go ahead."

"Now, if I don't hear from you in one week, then I'll go solo without your interview. I'll tell everything you told me."

"Fair enough."

"By the way, is there a good place to eat around here? I didn't have any breakfast."

AREA 51, NEVADA

Agent Freeman took the call on the Washington hotline at a comfortable chair inside a windowless room.

"Freeman, here."

"Did you find him?"

"No, sir. Not yet. We have our agents fanned out. We're checking all the major airports. The roads. Car rentals. Bus stops. Train stations. Ditches."

"Find him!"

"We will, sir."

NEEDLES

Norris watched Turner race away in his Camaro, then he too—in his sunglasses, t-shirt, shorts, and runners—left the motel on foot to the car rental he had picked at random in the phone book. Luckily, it was only a block away.

He swung the glass door open.

"It's great to be American, isn't it?" the young lady at the counter said. A TV set was behind her, the live broadcast of the moon landing on.

"Yes, isn't it," Norris answered, leaving his sunglasses over his eyes, glancing over his shoulder for a moment at the lot full of cars. "Man, it's hot out there."

The last thing she cared about was the heat. "How about that. We're on the moon."

"Yeah. It's. . . exciting," he said, with blank emotion. "I need a car, young lady."

"That's what we're here for, sir. Any particular car."

"I saw that new Plymouth hardtop out front. That should do the job."

"The blue Fury?"

"That's the one."

"I'll grab the paperwork." Her hand went under the counter and it came out with a form. "Name, please?" She glanced back at the lunar landing.

Norris knew he wouldn't dare give his real name. He removed his sunglasses and showed her the phony driver's license he had made at Area 51. "Ryan Smith."

On the other side of town, Agent Butler finished a quick greasy lunch at a Route 66 diner and paid an old man at the counter, then turned around to leave. There in the booth was Blake Turner, drinking coffee.

Turner looked up, and Butler turned away. No one could mistake that face. Or at least he thought it was Blake Turner. Butler walked out and into his car. He looked back to the restaurant, slowly. Turner glanced over.

Turner, huh? He was a long way from LA.

AREA 51

Freeman answered the ringing phone, almost pulling it off the chord.

"Freeman."

"It's Butler, sir."

"Where the hell have you been?"

"I just missed Norris by maybe thirty or forty minutes."

"Where?

"Needles. He rented a car from a local agency. He fit the description that the counter girl gave me. He's going by the name of Ryan Smith and he's driving a 1969 Plymouth Fury hardtop. Blue. Plate number J1926. The girl said he was headed for Arizona."

"Good. I'll send some men that way."

"You don't want me going with them?"

"No. I want you to head to Mexico, just in case. He could try to make a dash over the border."

"If you say so."

"Yes, I do."

"One other thing, sir."

"What? I'm busy."

"I saw Blake Turner in a restaurant on Route 66, west out of town."

"Turner? Who's he?"

"Blake Turner, the radio blabbermouth. You know, the guy who hates the war. I'd know those Hollywood looks anywhere."

"Oh, *him.* The dumb shit! What a kook! He thinks we killed Kennedy. One of those conspiracy theorists. OK, you saw Turner. So?"

"Kind of a coincidence, don't you think?"

"You think there's a connection?"

"I don't know for sure. Maybe."

"Look, just get going to Mexico."

"Yes, sir."

"I'll take care of Turner."

"I may need some backup."

"I'll send a couple men to the roads going south from Needles and a few more at the border crossings."

NEEDLES

Outside the car rental, Butler opened his map on the dash of the black Buick and contemplated his plan. If Norris was making a run to Mexico, then he'd have to take Highway 95 out of Needles. After that he could try side roads, but would probably end up in Blythe, one of the few towns between Needles and the Mexican border.

If Blythe was the target, he'd better step on it. Norris had at least a half-hour lead.

SOUTH OF NEEDLES

On a dusty side road, Norris removed the envelope containing the Area 51 photos from his suitcase. No sign of animals or humans or cars anywhere. He lit a match and burned the entire contents in the ditch, watching until the papers became cinders. Then he threw sand on top to cover everything. He glanced around at the desolate countryside of sand and rock, the sun bearing down on him. Sweat trickled off his forehead, onto his nose. He saw a deserted ranch approximately two hundred yards to the west. Far to the east, a river glittered in the sunshine. He produced a California map from the glove box and studied it against the driver's window. It had to be the Colorado, which separated Arizona from California. Norris had the option of two roads to the Mexican border. Two good roads, according to the map. *Paved. Or at least oiled.* Better than this buckboard of a dirt path. Finally, he determined, he could make his run into Mexico where California, Mexico, and Arizona converged west of Yuma.

He wiped his dry mouth. He was breathing heavy, his asthma acting up. Ninety miles to go.

He ran his finger down the paper. The California towns of Blythe and Ripley were ahead. He'd get on a good road there. He was dying of thirst. He'd grab a soda there, too. He shook his head. *Why didn't he buy a few Cokes in Needles?*

He jumped into his now-dusty Plymouth Fury hardtop and proceeded south.

Outside Blythe

Butler was flying down the straight-as-an-arrow dirt road towards the town when he saw a car five hundred yards ahead. There was no dust trail behind. Someone stood outside the back bumper. As Butler drew closer, he could see that the person was probably fixing a flat on the rear driver's side. Butler slowed down.

Oh, Geez. It's a Plymouth Fury. Blue. That much he could tell from a good distance away. He knew his cars. Someone in shorts was bent over the back wheel. Closer now, Butler saw the plate J1926. He pressed on the brakes and bolted from the car. The driver stood, looking around, stepping back. Butler recognized him.

"Norris!"

The man didn't speak.

"Norris," Butler repeated, softly, removing his gun from his chest holster. He pointed the barrel squarely at the startled Norris from ten feet away. "Hands up. CIA. Put down the tire iron."

Los Angeles

That evening, Blake Turner arrived at the WBID station by seven and considered the night's program inside his office, sipping a coffee. He'd talk about the moon landing, of course. What else? It was on everyone's mind. He'd been watching it on television all day long. Buzz, or whatever the hell his real name was, probably wouldn't be calling tonight. Unless he made it out of the country today. That story would be a great follow up. *Imagine,* he chuckled, *the Americans faking the moon landing.*

His office phone rang. His first thought was Buzz. . . from Mexico, but he was disappointed when he heard Mona, the front desk woman, say, "Mr. Turner, someone is here to see you."

"Who?"

"A man."

"Who is he?"

The woman's voice seemed tense. "He's with the government."

"Well. . . tell him to get lost."

"He told me to tell you that it's urgent."

"I don't want to see him."

Mona's voice was muffled now, as if others were in the lobby and were not supposed to hear. "Mr. Turner, I saw his badge. He's with the CIA."

Turner had received crazy phone calls before. Threatening phone calls from individuals and organizations, not to mention the outlandish letters. But this was different. *The CIA right here at the station.*

"Sir? He's waiting."

"Send him up."

The tap of shoes in the hall announced his arrival.

"Mr. Turner." The CIA man flashed his ID.

Turner was sitting behind his desk. "That's me."

The man returned his pocket ID to his suit breast pocket. "I'm Ronald Fuller. CIA." Fuller was the picture of conservatism. Dark suit, white shirt, dark tie, he was a husky man, about thirty-five.

"Can I get you a coffee? It's fresh."

"No thank you. Just had one."

"So. What yuh want with me, Mr. Fuller?"

"May I sit down?"

"Sure, pal, go ahead. Look, if this is about the JFK assassination thing, please don't bother. I'm not the only one who—"

Fuller waved a hand, closed the door, then found a chair. "No it's not about that. It's Norman Norris."

"Never heard of him."

"The man you met today in Needles. Let me refresh your memory. He called himself Buzz."

Turner leaned forward. "OK, I get it. I thought someone was glaring at me in the restaurant. By the way, you packing a rod?"

"I always carry a gun with me." Fuller slid back his suit jacket, enough for Turner to see a chest holster and a portion of the gun.

"OK, spit it out. What's in the wind? Why are you here?"

Fuller folded his hands. "We caught Norris. And he told us everything."

Turner learned long ago in this business to never admit anything. "Yeah? What did he tell you?"

"The conversation you two had at the motel on Route 66, across from the Red Lion. I guess I'll have to refresh your memory."

"Yes, you will."

"First off, he told you of Area 51."

"Big deal. I've heard of it before."

"Then he told you of the sound stage, that it was too dangerous to go to the moon and we'd have to fake it. He told you about Gus Grissom, the Russians too far ahead of us in space technology, the Van Allen Radiation Belts, the space suits too flimsy, and last but not least, he said he was going to call you from Mexico and that he would spill the beans on your radio show. Am I right?"

"OK, OK. I get the picture, pal. You want me to keep quiet."

"Yes."

"Why?"

"National Security."

Turner laughed. "Where have I heard that before?"

"The CIA, Washington, even the President wants you to keep quiet for another reason. That sound stage, all the details that he related to you, are the fakes. We really did land on the moon."

"What!"

Fuller smiled, standing. "We faked the whole thing to lay a trap for Norris. We had suspected spies in NASA for the last year. By faking the sound stage and everything else that went with it, we managed to weed Norris out. He's been working for the Russians. And his getaway proved it."

"Yeah, but. . . if he's a spy, why did he come to me?"

"What better way to show it was a fake, advertise it for the world to pick up on."

Turner slumped in his chair. He stared at Fuller. "So, you're telling me that we went to the moon after all?"

"Yes. That's why you can't say anything about this to anybody. If you say anything over the air, we'll come for you."

Turner stood. He was two feet away from the CIA agent. "Is that a threat?"

"Take it however you want. While I'm here, let me give you some advice."

"What's that?"

"Never miss a good chance to shut up. Goodbye, Mr. Turner."

12

Achtung, Thunderbolt!

Some people who lived through the Second World War—especially the veterans—never were completely able to shake it from their minds. For two such veterans who were on opposite sides during the conflict, Route 66 was their final showdown.

East Anglia, England—July, 1944

Lieutenant Ken Reed was the second last pilot through the open door of the briefing room of 405th Fighter Group. He looked around, then sat with four others he knew on wooden chairs in the middle of the large metal Quonset hut. The entrance door shut behind him. He chatted a bit with the pilots, who kidded him about always being last for everything. Last one to get out of bed in the hut. The last one to get dressed. The last one to eat. What they couldn't figure out was how could someone like that be near the top of the squadron in kills.

An officer climbed the stage and called out, "Attention!" Then he stepped aside to face an easel with a black curtain draped over it.

The pilots rose as one. Down the aisle marched three men, the Group CO, the mission leader, and the weather officer. The CO took the steps and turned to the fighter group. "At ease, gentlemen."

The men sat down. At the same time, the first officer pulled back on the black curtain. Reed and the other pilots followed the colored ribbons on the map of England and France to the targets of the day inside France. There were two today. Both roads. One was southwest of Calais. The other southeast of Calais.

"The first of today's two objectives, men, are the German Panzers that have been sitting at Calais for the last few weeks. The first group made their move at daybreak. We believe their destination is Normandy. We can't let them get there, gentlemen. They are taking this road." The CO tapped the mark with a wooden pointer. "We don't know, as yet, if there is any German fighter cover for the panzers. So, be on the alert. The second target is this area," he tapped the pointer again at the other spot, "where you will provide fighter support for an army unit in the process of taking a bridge."

The CO's message was short and sweet. He nodded at the missions leader, who advanced on the stage. He cleared his throat and began. "The 522nd Squadron will be taking on the panzers."

Reed sat up and took note. The 522nd was his squadron.

NEAR CALAIS, FRANCE

The German Panzer column chugged down the dusty road in the open country, the beaches of Normandy their destination. *What had taken them so long to finally move out?* thought tank commander Karl Spiller, in the middle of the pack. He poked his head through the hatch to glance around at the deadly German Army machinery. His alert eyes shot from horizon to horizon over the long grass of the open French country. He was struck by the power of the force he belonged to. This was one of the three prestigious panzer divisions of the German Fifteenth Army who had sat on their butts for weeks at Calais, across the English Channel, twenty miles from Dover, England, where General Patton and the Allies were supposed to come from. But Patton didn't show. *Why?* Because the Allies fooled them, Spiller concluded. That's why. The Allies landed at Normandy, instead. Far away from Calais. Where they were least expected. Had the Panzer Division been allowed loose at the start of it, they would have clobbered the Allies at Normandy. And the invasion never would have gotten hold. He just hoped they weren't too late now.

"Achtung, Thunderbolt!" someone shouted.

Spiller looked to the skies. There, banking tightly to the east, were two metallic American P-47 Thunderbolt fighters. They were in a two-plane element. Leader and wingman. Seventy feet apart. Spiller and the others had been briefed about the P-47s. Besides eight .50 caliber guns, each fighter often carried bombs and/or rockets. One thing was for certain. . . black-and-white D-Day stripes both sides of the wings. He caught the markings on one. 2K-M. One of the planes sped further down the column. But the other pilot banked the opposite way, coming around astern. From a far distance, Spiller could see a blob of some-thing under each side of the wide wing. Bombs! The pilot was lining up for a bombing run on the tanks. Spiller watched in shock as the pilot raced towards them and let go one bomb. . . then the other. The tank commander had no time to alert his crew below. The first blast hit! Then the second bomb struck the right side of the tank, throwing Spiller clean into the ditch.

Spiller landed in mud and water. He tried to crawl out, but was too groggy. He saw the P-47 turn and bank ahead, then come around and straight for him and others in the column who had managed to get out of their tanks. The pilot, with his bombs gone, began a strafing run. Wing guns blazing red blinks, the .50-caliber bullets tore a path right for Spiller.

One of the shells stabbed Spiller in the right knee. In an instant, the Thunderbolt raced only a few feet overtop, still firing at the ducking tank men down the line. . . then was gone almost as quickly as it showed up. Spiller tried to stand. . . and finally made it to his feet.

Then. . . the other P-47 screamed by, sputtering its guns as it went.

FLAGSTAFF, ARIZONA—OCTOBER 5, 1984

Ken Reed stood for his son as he entered the hangar office at the airport.

"Rick!"

"Hi, dad."

Reed bear-hugged his oldest boy, who had turned thirty-seven two days before. "When yuh get in?"

"Just drove up."

"You haven't been home?"

"Nope."

Reed looked over his son's shoulder. "Where's Katie and Carol?"

"In the hangar. They sent me to get you."

Reed poked his head around the corner. "Brenda, I'm stepping out for a bit," he said to the middle-aged company secretary. "You remember my son, Rick. He's up from San Diego."

"Hi, again, Rick," she said. "Good to see you. How's the weather in California?"

"Sunshine," Rick answered, politely.

"Mr. Reed? What if Mr. Hunter calls from Seattle?"

"Take down the information. I'll get back to him tomorrow."

"He's not in this Friday, remember, Mr. Reed?"

"Oh, yeah. What would I do without you, Brenda?"

"I shudder to think, sir," she replied, smiling.

Beyond the office, Reed met and hugged his daughter-in-law, Carol, and grand-daughter, Katie, then led them all on a tour of the immaculately clean hangar that housed Reed's thriving business, Reed Air Freight. Two medium-sized twin-engine props were in the middle of the hangar, the latest additions to the fleet of four. However, it was the aircraft in the corner that Rick's family were anxious to see—the Republic P-47 Thunderbolt fighter, the vintage American fighter plane from World War II that the elder Reed had bought for next to nothing in 1980 and had brought to full flying condition in three years. Resembling a flying tank, it was the same make and model aircraft Ken Reed had flown during the war, a D-version.

Affectionately tagged the "Jug" during the war, the Thunderbolt was a heavy fighter with a chunky nose, polished metal skin, and a huge, 4-bladed, 13-foot-long prop. In the war, she was built to punish. Eight non-functioning .50-caliber guns protruded off the leading edge of the wing. For the sake of passengers that Reed was licensed to carry, the only major modification to it—outside of some engine features—was an extra seat fitted snugly behind the cockpit seat.

"The D-Day stripes on the wing look great, dad."

Reed beamed with joy. "Yeah, it does. Just the way I remember mine. Perfect for next weekend. I hear you're staying till then."

"Yeah, if you don't mind us hanging around?"

"Do I still get a ride in it, grandpa, like you promised?" asked fourteen-year-old Katie, excited.

"You sure will. Tomorrow."

"Wicked!"

"I got a treat for you. We're going over the Grand Canyon."

"Wow!"

Rick and Carol exchanged uncomfortable glances.

"Oh, no. Dad, are you sure about the Canyon? The air traffic there is—"

"Relax, Rick." Reed was almost hit over the Canyon a month before. "It was the helicopter pilot at fault. He didn't stick to the flight plan. How was I supposed to know he'd turn onto my route?"

"Be careful," Carol said.

Reed winked at his pretty grand-daughter.

"I'll see you back at the house."

"OK, you guys. Give me another hour or so. I got a few things to do."

SEDONA, ARIZONA—OCTOBER 6

"Do you like it?" the bearded old man with the yellow teeth and German accent said to a young couple at the sidewalk art sale. Dozens of artists were selling their works this sunny Saturday morning. Painters and sculptors, mostly. Two specialized in charcoal.

"Yeah, I do," the man said. He studied the oil on canvas painting of an Arizona desert scene with Indians and red cliffs much like the powerful red-rock scenery surrounding Sedona. "You painted it?"

"Of course. My name is on it. Karl Spiller." The old man had a cigarette in his mouth. He plopped his newspaper, the *Phoenix Star*, on his folding chair, and limped closer to the two young people at the display table.

"You're quite good."

"Thank you," he said, with no emotion.

"Four hundred dollars, eh? I'll give you two hundred."

"Three hundred dollars and it is yours."

The woman nodded at her boyfriend. "Do it. It'll look nice in our den."

"All right, mister. It's a deal. Take a check?"

"I hope it is not out-of-state."

"No. I'm from Tucson."

"Write it up then."

A minute later, Karl Spiller took the check handed him without a word of thanks. Three hundred dollars should pay a bill or two. He sat back in his folding chair and let the golden sunshine beat down on his already-weathered skin of sixty-plus years. It was the first sale of the day. Two more paintings to go. He grabbed the newspaper and flipped to the WEEKEND section. The picture at the top of the page—a World

161

War II fighter and a pilot beside it—caught his immediate attention. He remembered the dreaded P-47 tank busters from the war. Through his reading glasses, he peered closer at the markings on the fighter. He could only make out the last letter—an M. The port wing hid the rest.

Coincidence?

He read the lines below the photo. It was about Route 66. In another week, Saturday, October 13, a big celebration was planned in Williams, Arizona, not far from Sedona. The last six miles of the road would be decertified. I-40 would be officially opened and Route 66 would be officially by-passed. The pilot—Ken Reed—and his P-47 were to do a fly-past that day. Media people from as far away as Los Angeles and Chicago would be there. Thousands in total were expected. Spiller's eyebrows twitched when he read that the pilot was a youthful-looking sixty-two, a former P-47 pilot in the American Eighth Air Force, the 405th Fighter Group, 522nd Squadron. His nickname during the war was "Crazy Kenny." Fourteen aerial kills, two trains, and six tanks. *Tanks!*

Apparently, Reed was a self-made millionaire who had made his fortune in Flagstaff real estate in the 1970s and now owned his own air freight company based in Flagstaff. The P-47 was his toy. He and the machine had been to air shows, on aerial tours, and even in a Hollywood movie.

Spiller slapped the newspaper closed. He burned with anger. Another American war vet who prospered after the war. Meanwhile, here he was barely making a living. His American-born wife took the two kids and left him ten years ago. It was his drinking, she claimed. The chain smoking didn't help too much either. *What did she know?* She hadn't gone through the war. At the time he was a machinist. He soon lost that job, too. As he did others before and since. An art student in Nazi Germany before the war, he always had a fondness for art. He came to Sedona in 1982. Broke, divorced, and full of cancer. He convinced himself he had to get away from it all and go back to his first love—painting. And the dry air was a tonic.

Trouble was, he was a starving artist, making only just enough to feed and clothe himself.

Reed drove to the airport, his grand-daughter in the front seat with him. They had just come from an early McDonald's lunch of hamburgers, fries, and shakes. They stopped behind the air freight hangar.

"Grandpa?" she asked, before they got out of the car.

"Yes, Katie, what is it?"

"How many Germans did you kill during the war?"

Reed was caught off-guard. His grand-daughter had never asked him anything so blunt about his fighter pilot days. She was growing up. "It's hard to say. Why would you ask?"

She shrugged. "Just... wondering."

"Kids asking you at school?"

"Yeah."

"It was war time, Katie. Sometimes you have to do things you don't like. As a pilot I had the advantage of not seeing my enemy face to face. I had fourteen kills in the air. A few of those parachuted out in time. Because, you see, we received the credit for shooting down the machine and not the person. I also hit some tanks and trains. There were people in those. So, I don't know. Maybe, all told, twenty. Twenty-five. Could even have been more. Look, tell your friends in school that I did what I had to do. We all did back then."

"Sure, grandpa."

"Now, let's go for a ride."

"On one condition" She grinned at him.

"Boy, you really are growing up. What condition is that?"

"Grandma said you weren't supposed to charge me like you do the others that you take to the Canyon."

Reed laughed. "OK. I won't."

Reed left the runway heading west, the 2300 horsepower radial engine roaring at 160 miles per hour. He and his passenger stuck to their seats by the torque, he reached down and flicked a switch that sucked the undercarriage into the wing. He advanced the throttle, climbed and leveled out at a thousand feet. Even throttling back, the engine noise was still deafening.

"You all right back there, Katie!" Reed turned his head and shouted over his shoulder to Katie behind him in a thick waist-coat.

"Just fine, grandpa. That was fun!"

"Are you cramped?"

"No."

"If you think the take-off was fun, just wait till I show you something. But don't you dare tell your mom and dad. OK?"

"OK, grandpa!"

"You won't turn upside-down will you?"

"Oh, no. Nothing like that."

Reed banked right and followed old Route 66 for a few miles, then No. 180 Highway to the junction of the No. 64. There, he banked right one more time and out away from the highway to the direction of the Grand Canyon. This was desolate, flat country with short, parched grass. Not too much else growing, except for the occasional dry bush here and there. A couple of ranches were scattered about to the far left. Six miles ahead, he could see his friend's ranch, out in the open by itself.

"Here we go, Katie!"

Reed shoved the stick forward until he was down to two hundred feet. He leveled off. . . then nudged the stick ever so slightly until his altitude read forty feet. . . then thirty. . . then twenty-five. No other buildings, cars or people were around for miles. The ranch was dead ahead. He pushed the throttle forward.

"Go, grandpa! Go!" Katie screamed from the back seat.

At three hundred miles per hour, he aimed the P-47 for the one-hundred-foot gap between the house and the empty corral. The horses were in the barn, the other side of the house. At the last second, he saw someone come out to the porch off to the right side. Reed raced by, waggling his wings in jerky motions, his huge prop only a few feet off the ground.

On the porch, Charlie Witting waved to his long-time friend of forty years. They had enlisted together the same day in 1942. Reed with the Air Force. Witting with the Army. Both ended up in the European Theater of Operations.

Witting's plump wife came running out the door. "*What the hell was that?*" she gasped, fighting for air. "*The dishes shook.*"

Witting glanced at his wife, his attention quickly returning to the shiny P-47, now climbing to the north. "Ah, just Crazy Kenny," he grinned.

"Geez, why does he have to do that? It scares the animals half to death. One of these times somebody's going to report him."

Reed climbed, banked left and leveled out at one thousand feet as if nothing out of the ordinary had occurred.

"There it is, Katie!" Reed pointed ahead. "The Grand Canyon. I hope you'll like it from the air."

"I'm sure I will."

Karl Spiller arrived at the Flagstaff airport a few minutes before Reed and his grand-daughter landed. From inside his beat-up 1977 Dodge Aspen, Spiller watched the P-47 taxiing to the aircraft's dispersal spot outside the hangar. He saw the markings on the World War II fighter. . . and burned inside.

He emerged from his car, stamped his cigarette into the gravel, and crossed the road, limping all the way.

Reed stomped onto the Thunderbolt's wing and helped his grand-daughter out of the cockpit. He jumped to the concrete first, taking Katie's hand, and eased her down.

"I'm still buzzing," she said.

"Are you, OK? You're not dizzy, are you?" He unzipped his leather flight jacket with the wool collar.

"No, nothing like that, grandpa. It seems like the ground's still moving."

Reed smiled.

"Remember, don't tell your parents."

"I won't."

"Tell them what?"

Reed and Katie turned quickly, startled.

"Who are you?" Reed asked the man with the gray beard.

"That is some fighter you have."

"Thank you." Reed detected a German accent of war veteran age.

"I read about you. You flew P-47s in the war?"

"Yes, I did."

The man rubbed his chin. "Not as graceful as the ME-109."

"But it got the job done."

"If that is how you wish to rationalize it."

"What do you mean by that?"

"Those fuselage markings, do they signify anything?"

Reed glanced at Katie, then back to the unsmiling German. "Yes. 2K-M was the same as I used in the war. 405th Fighter Group, Eighth Air Force." He put his hand on his grand-daughter's shoulder. "Were you in the war?"

"Yes. Panzers. Western Front in France. That's where I got this limp." The man smiled thinly, at best. "Bullet in the leg."

"Sorry."

Spiller ignored Reed's sympathy. "I came to see it up close. I have not seen a Thunderbolt. . . since. . . a long time ago." He grunted. "Thanks."

"You're welcome."

When the man slipped away, Katie said to her grandfather, "What are panzers, grandpa?"

"German tanks," he answered. "And I have to admit that their tanks were better than ours."

"I don't think he liked you," she scowled.

Reed frowned. That was an understatement. "Of course not. I shot up a few German tanks."

"Wouldn't that be something if you shot up *his* tank?"

"Come on, Katie, that would be too much of a coincidence. Let's go have a cool can of soda. You wanna Coke?"

"How about Pepsi?"

In the Mercedes, Reed checked his rear-view mirror as he turned the corner to his block. He steered into the driveway and glared over his shoulder at the Dodge Aspen passing by.

"Isn't that the German?" Katie said, recognizing the driver hunched over the wheel.

Reed nodded. "Yeah, it is."

"Do you think he followed you home?"

"I dunno."

"There's something odd about him, grandpa."

"I think we'd better keep this to ourselves, too. Let's go in the house."

Katie and her grandfather forgot about the ornery German as best they could during the coming week. There was too much to do, Rick's family was on vacation, and Reed was preparing the Thunderbolt for his fly-past over Williams at high noon on Saturday. That Saturday morning, he had a late breakfast with the entire family in his ranch-style house.

Over his eggs at the eat-in kitchen table, he reminisced. "I can't believe it. Route 66 at an end. The Feds are closing down the last six miles. The interstates have taken over. You know, I had my first road lesson on Route 66."

"I didn't know that," Rick said.

"Yep. . . 1941 it was. My father's old purple Mercury with the suicide doors. I got my license two months later. A month after that came Pearl Harbor and the war. It'll be a shame to see Route 66 go for good. A lot of fond memories. Drive-ins. Diners. Driving my first car out to California. Those hairpin turns at Oatman, near the border. I was never so damn scared in my life."

"Once was enough for me," Reed's wife, Janet, added. "I shut my eyes the whole time."

"The new road avoided all that," Reed continued. "No character to these interstates."

"That's progress, dad," Rick said. "The traffic has to move."

"Suppose so. Still though, it's a shame. And it sure seemed to happen fast. There was Route 66, busy as hell, then the interstates came, and nothing on Route 66. It died."

"Come on, pop. Cross-country, two-lanes don't cut it anymore. After a few years, nobody will think twice about Route 66. It's a dinosaur."

Reed eyed his watch. He had to get to the airport. He glanced at Katie. "We best be going."

"OK, grandpa. Let's roll."

"Katie," Janet said, frowning, "you've been around your grandfather too long."

"Take it easy, dad?" Carol asked. "For Katie's sake."

"Yeah," Rick added. "Nothing wild."

"Relax, you two. It's only a fly-past. It's more fun with a passenger." Reed made a toothy grin. "Besides, she wants to go. And secondly, she's the only one in the family that's skinny enough to fit in the seat." He winked at Katie.

Reed and Katie walked towards the shiny Thunderbolt at the far corner of the hangar near the large open door. Together, they pulled the propeller through sixteen blades by hand in order to circulate the oil before start-up. In the old days of the war, P-47s had to be started by an external power source. Reed changed that for convenience as well as for safety by switching to the more modern magnetos.

"All set?" Reed asked her.

Suddenly, Karl Spiller limped around the corner and came within a few feet of Reed.

"You again," Reed said, unfriendly. He was not happy about seeing the bad-tempered German, who smelled badly of body odor and cigarette smoke. "Long time no see. You know, I never did get your name."

"I hear you're taking on a passenger today."

"Yes. My grand-daughter."

"I want you to take *me*."

"You! Why you? No. . . look, pal, I said I was taking my grand-daughter, here."

Spiller startled Reed and Katie by pulling a pistol out of his jacket and pointing the barrel at Reed. . . then Katie. . . then back to Reed. "You are taking me."

"Now, hold on there, fellah," Reed said, calmly, not to frighten his grand-daughter. "Put the gun down. Don't do anything you may regret."

Spiller looked around. "If either of you makes a warning sound, your grandpa here gets it. You understand, girl?"

Katie nodded, the rest of her body frozen stiff. She tried to speak, but found she couldn't.

"What's this all about?"

"You, Mr. Reed, bombed my tank back in the war in France. A few weeks after your D-Day, as they call it. And if that was not enough, you strafed us as we were running. I took a bullet from you in the leg. And I have had this blasted limp ever since. I know it was you because I remember the markings. 2K-M. You said those were yours during the war. Right? It was you, was it not? Well, was it, damnit! Do you remember? No, you probably do not because you shot up so many."

Katie sucked in air. "It was war," she said.

"Shut up, little girl. What do you know?"

"What did you expect my grandfather to do?"

"I said, shut up!"

"Bastard!"

"Hush, Katie," Reed begged her. "Leave her out of this whoever you are."

"The name is Spiller. Karl Spiller."

"OK, Spiller, get to the point. What the hell's your beef?"

"I am getting in the cockpit, Reed, and we are going for a little ride," he said with conviction, the barrel still pointed towards Reed. "Any warning and you get it."

"You've made that very clear, pal."

"Now, let us go. And you," Spiller said to the girl, "you stay right where you are until we are in the air. Better yet, come out to the door where I can see you after. If I see you move, your grandpa fighter pilot is dead. I will be watching right up until take-off. Do you understand me?"

Katie swallowed. "Yes, I do." She looked at her grandpa, who winked at her. She tried to smile, but couldn't.

Reed said to Katie, "Do what the man says and stay right where you are." Then lifted one eyebrow. It was a signal.

Katie took this to mean, but once he leaves the runway. . . make a B-line for the nearest telephone.

Spiller climbed into the fighter cockpit first and sat down, the barrel on Reed the whole time. "Move it!"

Reed got up and seated himself directly in front of Spiller.

"Start this monster up."

Reed climbed in and engaged the starter until the powerful radial engine cranked and caught fire, sending out a cloud of blue smoke. Katie plugged her ears as the engine ran roughly at first, then quickly smoothed out until the smoke dispersed. Reed unlocked the tail wheel, put the flaps up, and pulled the World War II fighter away.

"FLAGSTAFF TOWER, THIS IS 2K-M, REQUESTING TAKE-OFF PROCE-DURES," he said into his radio transmitter.

"YOU ARE CLEARED FOR TAKE-OFF ON RUNWAY TWO-SEVEN."

"ROGER, TOWER."

Reed turned onto the selected runway and braked the fighter. He glanced over his shoulder.

"There is a gun at your head!" Spiller shouted.

"I know. I just want to know where we're going?"

"Williams. Where else? Let us go."

Reed rolled forward to center the tail wheel. Then he locked it. He pressed the brakes and advanced the throttle to 30 inches of manifold pressure. He released the brakes. . . and they were off. Reed then advanced the power to 51 inches manifold pressure. He brought the tail up. Lots of runway left. They climbed into the air at 165 miles per hour. Reed checked his gauges. Everything fine.

Rick, Carol, and Janet were standing in a parking lot near the Williams main drag through town that had been Route 66 for decades. Thousands were in attendance. During a break in speeches from a podium, they looked up when they heard and saw the Thunderbolt approaching a little more than a mile away at under three hundred feet.

"Here comes, dad."

"Now, Yank, you will fly it right into the crowd," Spiller shouted.

"So, that's your game, is it?" Reed replied as loudly as he could. "Pissed off at the world. Couldn't cope with losing the war. And don't forget the dickhead of a leader you had. Adolf Fucking Hitler."

"Do it!" Spiller stuck the gun into Reed's temple.

"Go to hell!"

Instead, Reed flipped the fighter completely over until it was upside down. Reed glanced down at the bubble canopy and saw the gun on the glass, as he flashed by the assembled crowd only a hundred feet below. He reached out and grabbed the weapon before Spiller could and stuck it under his right thigh.

Reed backed off on the throttles making Spiller bang forward against the back of Reed's seat. Reed leaned to the right side and elbowed Spiller hard to the face. *Take that, buster!* Not once, but three times. *Now this asshole was going to receive the ride of his life.* To keep Spiller off-balance, Reed quickly flipped the machine right-side up, then banked severely to the left. Coming out of it, he banked right, twisting and turning. He climbed. . . then he dropped like a rock.

Never the same thing for too long. All within sight of the Route 66 crowd.

Spiller didn't know what hit him. He finally started to vomit all over the cockpit and glass.

Reed made a face. It was a good thing he had a strong stomach.

On the ground, Rick stood flabbergasted, looking straight up. "Mom, what the hell is dad doing?"

"Oh, God, Ken." She gulped. "I don't know, Rick. The mayor told him only a fly-past."

"Some fly-past. Crap! I didn't think a Thunderbolt could do those maneuvers."

"Never mind that! My baby's in there!" Carol screamed.

When it looked like Spiller had had enough, Reed elbowed him two more times for good measure. With Spiller seemingly knocked out for the time being, Reed knew he had to get this bird down as soon as possible. He followed Route 66 east to Flagstaff. Ahead was a field near a stretch of old Route 66, outside Flagstaff. He aimed for it. . . hoping the ground wouldn't be too soft. . . but at the last moment landed on the old highway, instead.

Reed brought the machine to a full halt in the middle of the white stripes. He shut the radial engine off, the prop whining until it came to a stop. In the distance a car was fast approaching. He climbed down the wing, leaving Spiller unconscious in the rear seat.

A blue-and-white car roared up to the fighter. It was the Arizona State Police. Guns drawn, two officers jumped out. And so did Katie from the back seat.

"Grandpa!"

Katie ran to Reed's outstretched arms. They embraced tightly.

"Are you all right, grandpa?"

"I'm fine. I can't say the same for the other guy."

They watched the policeman climb the fighter and pull Spiller out by his coat collar.

"What a mess," one of the officers said.

"What happened to him?" Katie asked, suspiciously.

Reed shook his head. "Some people just can't take flying." Reed turned to his grand-daughter. "You called the State Police? That was smart thinking, Katie." He smiled at her.

She blushed. "Thanks."

"Wait'll the media gets hold of this story. You wanna get into the papers?"

"Sure."

Reed leaned closer to Katie and said, "I just hope I don't get charged with landing on a public road."

Epilogue

The truck driver brought the big red-and-white Coca-Cola semi to a
stop a few car lengths ahead of two people beside a black Mazda sports
car. The couple hurried up to the passenger side of the cab.

The driver slid over in the bench seat and pushed the button to lower
the power-window. "Yuh all right?" he said to a man and woman a good
two generations younger than he was.

Both wore shorts this warm, dry day. The man was blonde and husky,
full of freckles. She was a frizzy-permed brunette who wore a tight,
low-cut T-shirt she had probably been poured into. Nothing was left
to the imagination.

"It's kind of embarrassing," the man confessed, mildly.

"Ran outta gas, did yuh?"

"Yeah, we did," the man laughed, relieved to admit what they had
done. "I thought we'd make it to Albuquerque with what we had, but
we came up a few miles short. I should have filled up near the Indian
reserve."

"Well, yuh got close. Yuh missed the outskirts by about six miles."

"There isn't much around here, is there?"

"No, there isn't. Dust and mountains. So, got a can with yuh?"

"In the trunk."

"Get it. I'll drive you into Albuquerque."

"Really? That's awfully nice of you," the woman said.

"Ah, don't mention it. Come on."

173

The man snatched the can from their trunk, and he and the woman climbed into the air-conditioned cab, the woman between the two men. The driver was a bald, skinny, sixtyish old man with a pony tail, who looked like a left-wing university professor from the 70s. Although his weather-beaten skin looked like leather, he had a youthful expression and a friendly ease about him.

"I'm Brett Conway from Oklahoma City. You?" The driver took the last swallow of his decaf coffee and placed the empty on the dash drink pad beside his cell phone.

"We're the Courtneys," the husky man said. "I'm Tim and this is my wife, Barb."

"Hi, yuh." Conway ran through the gears, getting the rig up to fifty miles an hour. "Where yuh from?"

"San Bernardino, California."

"Hey, nice spot. Sure has changed the last few years. LA has caught up to it."

"Been that way for quite a while, I'm told."

"What yuh do fer a living?"

"I'm a teacher," Barb answered, looking straight ahead at the bleak countryside. "Fifth grade."

"Noble profession."

"Thanks."

"Right now, I'm helping out my husband."

"Yeah, doing what?"

"I'm a writer," Tim answered for himself.

"No kidding?"

"The *San Bernardino Star*. News. Once a week a column on Wall Street. Mutual Funds. It's ghost written because I'm not licensed for giving financial advice. I do a lot of freelance stuff, too. A couple of novels. Some magazine pieces. For the next couple weeks I'm doing an article for *Performance Cars Magazine*."

"I heard of them. Lots of beefed up '55 Chevys with small blocks."

"Right. I'm working on a diary for them."

"A diary? On what?" Conway asked.

"We're cruising old Route 66. The whole way. As best we can, anyway. It's still supposed to be about eighty percent drivable. We'll have to take some detours here and there."

Conway smiled. "That's right. Got a good guide? You'll need one."

"Sure do. Tom Snyder's book."

"I know it. Read it cover to cover, twice. Quite a few people take the old Route 66 every year. Seems to be a trendy thing to do. Actually, that's what I'm doing here, too. Every so often, I get off I-40 and take the road for old time's sake. I drove it for years between Chicago and Los Angeles before the interstates came."

"How long have you been driving semis?" Barb asked.

"Over forty years. Since 1955. I met my wife on the road, actually. She was hitch-hiking near Amarillo, the summer of 1960. By the time we made it to Los Angeles, we were married."

Tim was surprised. "That fast, huh?"

"We're still together and she's still as pretty as the day I married her."

"I think that's romantic," Barb said. "You like truck driving?"

"Every minute of it. Kind of sad they closed Route 66 down, though."

"Why sad?" Tim wanted to know. "The four lanes are quicker, especially for a truck driver like yourself. Time is money."

"Yeah, I know. It's. . . well. . . something was lost when they shut her down for good. I know what yuh mean, though. Route 66 became a fat old lump. Oops, fat isn't politically-correct anymore, is it?"

"How about. . . delightfully plump," Barb said.

Conway laughed. "So, why did you folks decide to give 'er a go?"

"My great-grandparents drove it back in 1929," Tim said. "They were New Yorkers. They moved out to the West Coast and stayed. Drove the entire route from Chicago to Santa Monica in a brand-new Pierce Arrow my great-grandfather bought off a car lot in Chicago."

The truck driver whistled. "Holy, cow! Back in them days most of the road wasn't even paved." Then Conway thought of something. "Hold on a second. You said your last name was Courtney? You mean. . . like. . . the Courtney Inn?"

"The same."

"I know the place well. Right on Route 66, this side of San Bernardino before the Mojave Desert. I've stayed there a few times. Nice place. Great place to eat from what I can remember, although I haven't seen it for a few years. Do they still have the orange juice stand?"

"Oh, yeah. Going on seventy years now. That was something my great-grandparents started."

"Does your family still run the inn?"

"Nope. My father sold it in 1972. The new owners kept the name, though. They still manage to make a good buck, even though the interstate missed it."

The driver pointed. "There's the gas station. . . up ahead."

Conway stopped at the Mazda.

"Thanks a bunch for the ride," Tim said, climbing out the semi cab.

"And the conversation," Barb added.

"My pleasure. You have yourself a good day, now."

"Thanks. You, too."

The girl smiled her thanks.

Conway watched *Bouncing Barbie* leave out the passenger door. He remembered a few girls like that in his younger days.

The couple crossed the road.

Conway leaned his head out the window. "Don't forget. Keep at least half a tank at all times, especially through the next couple states."

"I will," Tim replied, the gas can held tight in his hand.

"Are you planning on stopping in Albuquerque?"

"Maybe. Why?"

"Lots of good places to eat, especially if you like Mexican. There's a real nice movie theater about a mile into town. The Metropolitan. They have "cheap night" tonight. The four-dollar movies. Good ones, too. Anyway, I better let yuh get on your way. Happy motoring. I hope you enjoy Route 66 as much as I did."

"We'll try."

"Oh. . . hey. . . wait. One last bit of advice."

"Sure. Shoot."

Conway smiled slowly. "Take your time. Don't rush it."

Acknowledgements

There's a few people I'd like to thank for helping me put this book together. First off, my brother, Greg, who introduced me to the many wonders of Route 66 during a vacation we spent together in Arizona in November 1999, in which we cruised the old open road between Seligman and Williams and bought some Route 66 souvenirs along the way. Then there was John and Beth Rose here in Burlington, Ontario, who drove a good portion of Route 66 between Chicago and LA and put on a great slide show for me and my son to show us.

Bob Moore and Paul Taylor of *Route 66 Magazine* supplied me with some facts here and there that I inserted into my stories. There's also Phillips Petroleum Company, which we know better as *Phillips 66*, especially Kathy Triebel, for going through the company's archives to dig out some valuable info on their long-gone but well-remembered Highway Hostesses. I can't forget Mike Wallis for his books and videos of Route 66. Although I've never met the man, he brought the old road to life for me and countless others.

Last, but not least, I'd like to thank my wife, Bonnie, for putting up with all my crazy ideas all these years.

Daniel Wyatt, Burlington, Ontario, Canada